HOW TO BE A
HERO
LAND of
LOST THINGS

To Steve, whose boat doesn't smell of toenails
C.W.

First published 2021 by Macmillan Children's Books
an imprint of Pan Macmillan
The Smithson, 6 Briset Street, London EC1M 5NR
EU representative: Macmillan Publishers Ireland Limited,
Mallard Lodge, Lansdowne Village, Dublin 4
Associated companies throughout the world
www.panmacmillan.com

ISBN 978-1-5290-4505-5

Text copyright © Cat Weldon 2021
Illustrations copyright © Katie Kear 2021

1 3 5 7 9 8 6 4 2

·HOW TO BE A· HERO

LAND of LOST THINGS

CAT WELDON

Illustrated by Katie Kear

MACMILLAN CHILDREN'S BOOKS

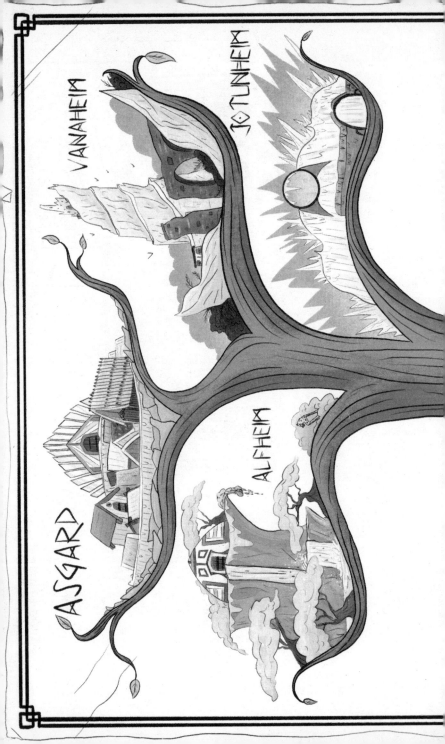

A Guide to the Nine Worlds
By Blood-Runs-Cold, Leader of the Valkyries

The Nine Worlds

Imagine the biggest tree you can. No, bigger than that.

BIGGER.

BIGGER.

That's Yggdrasil, and it makes your tree look like a bit of wilted broccoli. Nine whole worlds hang from Yggdrasil – *that's* how big it is.

Asgard: Right at the top, because it's the best. Home of the Gods and ruled over by Odin. In Asgard you can find *Valhalla*, Odin's Great Hall, where the greatest warriors come after they've died. There they can fight, feast and drink until *Ragnarok*, the battle at the end of the world. At Ragnarok they will be called upon to fight the Frost Giants for Odin, but until then it's basically party time.

Vanaheim: Home to the Gods who aren't cool enough to be in

Asgard. They're mostly interested in growing stuff; inhabitants of Asgard are more interested in fighting.

Alfheim: Home of the Elves. Yes, they have pointy ears. Yes, they giggle a lot. Mostly harmless, but keep them where you can see them.

Jotunheim: Home of the Giants, including our mortal enemies the Frost Giants. They keep trying to break into Asgard; we keep beating them in battle. Lots of mountains; good for skiing.

Midgard: This is where you can find living humans, living their ordinary lives, with ordinary horses, ordinary farms and ordinary families.

Svartalfheim: Home of the Dwarves. A maze of caves and mines. They love tinkering with gold and making magical gadgets.

Muspell: Land of Fire. Ruled over by Sutr, a Fire Giant. Nice saunas.

Helheim: Home of the Queen of the Dead, Hel. Yes, she named the place after herself. Tells you everything you need to know, really.

Niflheim: Land of the Unworthy Dead. The dragon Nidhogg

lives here and chews on the roots of the world tree. He likes poetry, gold and trampling anyone unlucky enough to be sent there.

Who's Who in Asgard

Odin: The Allfather, the Spear Shaker, the Terrifying One-Eyed Chief of the Gods. The boss.

Frigg: Goddess of Family. Odin's wife. Knows the future, but won't tell anyone.

Loki: The Trickster. Enjoys a 'joke'. Approach with caution. Technically a Fire Giant, but Odin lets him live in Asgard because they're blood brothers.

Thor: God of Thunder. Do not touch his hammer. Seriously.

Freyja: Goddess of Love and Sorcery. Likes cats. *I'm not kidding about the cats. She has cat ornaments, cat jewellery and is usually covered in cat hair. She even has a pair of giant cats for pulling her chariot.*

The Valkyries: Elite female warriors, Valkyries are servants of Odin, Chief of the Gods. They bring the greatest warriors and Heroes to Valhalla on their flying horses. At Ragnarok, the battle at the end of the world, they will lead the Gods and warriors of Valhalla in the final clash against the Frost Giants.

Travel between Worlds

It is possible to travel between worlds by flying or climbing through Yggdrasil's branches. Not easy, but possible. Only the Gods (and Valkyries) have really got the hang of it. The Giants have managed it a few times, more through luck than anything else.

Valkyries and Odin travel by flying horse, Loki has special shoes and Freyja uses a magic cloak. The Bifrost Bridge links Asgard and Midgard. When humans on Midgard see it, they call it a rainbow.

Magic

It's simple: magic can only be created by magical creatures – Dwarves, Elves and, to a certain extent, Giants. All other magic comes from magical objects *made* by magical creatures, usually the Dwarves.

Except for Odin: he learned how to do magic by hanging upside down from Yggdrasil for nine days to discover the secrets of the Runes. Fancy doing that? No? Then no magic for you.

Chapter One

Deadman's Cove

'HEAVE!'

A rope was pressed into Whetstone's hands and he joined the Vikings struggling to drag the longboat to shore. Rain lashed down on the massive hairy men, their boots

slipping on the pebbly beach. Inch by painful inch the boat crawled closer, fighting the wind and tide, which seemed determined to keep it out at sea.

Whetstone's boots slithered on the rocks, nearly sending him tumbling. He gripped on as the rope burned his pale hands. He didn't want to die in Deadman's Cove – it was far too predictable.

'COME ON – PUT YOUR BACKS INTO IT! WE'RE NEARLY THERE!' bellowed Awfulrick, the Viking Chief of Krud, his face red with effort. The waves pounded, mixing sea spray with rain to create a cold, salty soup.

'We'll never make it,' panted Whetstone, scrubbing salt water out of his eyes with his sleeve. 'It's too rough. You'd have to be mad to go out in weather like this.'

Awfulrick shrugged, Vikings weren't generally known for their sensible decision-making.

It was thanks to Whetstone that the longboat had been noticed at all. While mooching along the cliffs, he had spotted it clearly in trouble amongst the foaming waves. Whetstone had been looking for a way to get out of Krud for weeks now, but strange weather had plagued the village. This was the first and only boat he had seen, the powerful wind and raging tides keeping everything else away from the shore.

Out at sea the ship had looked tiny, tossed on the waves like a child's toy. But up close it was *huge* and dangerous. Sleek sides were lined with circular shields, and a carved dragon figurehead snarled from the front.

With the crunch of wood on shingle, the longboat reached the beach. The Vikings onboard jumped off, joining the effort to pull the boat above the high-water mark. Whetstone's heart thudded in his chest: this boat was going to be his ticket out of Krud. All he had to do was talk his way on to the crew, prove himself useful and . . .

'Get out of the way, weasel,' said Bragi, a young Viking with longish red hair and a biggish nose. He gave Whetstone a shove, knocking him into a rockpool.

'WHETSTONE!' Awfulrick bellowed. 'STOP MESSING ABOUT. GET BACK TO THE VILLAGE AND TELL ETHEL TO GET A STEW ON FOR OUR VISITORS!'

'Fine.' Whetstone pulled a nosey crab out of his tunic and tossed it away. Slimy seaweed clung to his hands; he sneakily wiped them on Bragi's cloak. 'It's not as if fighting with wet wood and getting covered in splinters is my idea of a good time.'

Dodging out of the way as the boat was dragged up the beach, Whetstone started the long trudge towards the cliffs and back to Krud. He would find an opportunity to speak to the longboat crew later, when everyone was dry and in a better mood.

At the top of the cliffs, Whetstone's spine prickled. He turned to look down on the scene below him. The ship was safely on the beach now, the crew hurriedly unloading chests as the rain bucketed down. But in the centre of the action one man stood motionless, watching Whetstone. A man who had the bushiest red beard the boy had ever seen.

Whetstone raised his hand in a wave. People often stared at Whetstone these days. Stories about his adventures had been spreading, and if he was lucky the sailors might have already heard of him – that would make convincing them to let him

9

join their crew easier. Wind caught what was left of the ragged sail and an image of a sea serpent with gaping jaws billowed. Whetstone shivered and lowered his hand, pulling his cloak in against the biting wind. He was sure he could still feel the eyes of the bearded man on him as he walked away.

❀

Back at the Great Hall, Whetstone was met by great excitement. Fires had been built into infernos, fresh sawdust was spread on the floor and someone had even brought out the *fancy* plates – you know, the ones without the gnaw marks. He nodded pointedly to Ethel and she dropped something scaly into the pot. The smell of fish rolled across the room catching in Whetstone's throat and making him cough.

The boy slid on to the bench furthest from the cauldron and tipped water out of his far-too-big boots, his mind still on the longboat and the strange, bearded man. The crew would be staying in Krud tonight, and tomorrow he could be on his way to start his quest. He had wasted too much time hanging around already. His stomach churned at the thought of getting on the boat. Whetstone told himself it was excitement, not queasiness. He was sure he wouldn't get seasick, not this time.

A few minutes later, just as Whetstone had started to dry out, Awfulrick led the visitors into the Great Hall. There were about thirty men, all tired and wet. They dropped on to benches gratefully, puddles soon forming by their feet as rain and seawater dripped off their hair and clothes. The man with the red beard caught Whetstone's eye and winked.

'LOVELY DAY FOR A SAIL!' bellowed Awfulrick, slamming a cup of mead into the man's hand.

The man nodded, his beard bouncing up and down. 'We had fair winds until we got within sight of Krud. You must've done something to anger Thor.'

Awfulrick laughed. 'IT'S NOT THOR WE HAVE TO WORRY ABOUT.' He peered around the room. 'WHETSTONE! GET UP HERE AND TELL THEM WHAT YOU DID TO THAT DRAGON!'

Whetstone froze midway through wringing water out of his cloak. Awfulrick's magical cup bounced up and down

on the Chief's shoulder like a

demented metal parrot. It squeaked and then began to speak
in a voice that sounded like a stuck cutlery drawer:

> *Whetstone came to Krud with a feeling*
> *That he just had to go stealing.*
> *He took this fine cup,*
> *But a colossal mix-up,*
> *Left him stranded in Asgard and reeling.*

> *A Valkyrie named Lotta was to blame,*
> *But Whetstone thought it a game.*
> *He was in for a shock,*
> *It was a long drop,*
> *To send him home once again.*

The crowd started to elbow each other and mutter. This story
was a firm favourite with the Vikings of Krud. A few of them
even started mouthing the words along with the cup.

> *Whetstone wanted to find Glory and Fame,*
> *To have us all knowing his name.*
> *So with Loki a deal he struck,*
> *To swap their freedom for Awfulrick's cup,*
> *But the Trickster was playing a game.*

Whetstone felt his heart speed up. He would still wake up in a
sweat remembering Loki's dark eyes and twisted smile.

Lotta agreed to help out with the quest;
She wanted to prove that she was the best.
They climbed down the tree,
But things weren't easy,
And they woke a dragon who wasn't impressed.

Whetstone swallowed his fears. He flattened his scruffy hair. He had always wanted to be famous – he just thought he would be a famous thief, not a Hero.

The dragon was looking for food;
A tasty Valkyrie and Viking would do.
But instead the cup was dinner,
Till our Hero played a winner,
Beating the dragon and Loki too!

The crowd burst into applause. A large hand clamped round the neck of Whetstone's tunic, yanking him out of his memories and also off the bench. Oresmiter, Awfulrick's second-in-command, wheeled the boy to the front of the hall, Whetstone's boots leaving long muddy streaks across the floor.

Awfulrick stood silhouetted in front of the fireplace, the cup gleaming on his shoulder. 'THERE YOU ARE!'

Oresmiter released the boy and the Vikings cheered. The longboat crew eyed him with interest.

'SLAYER OF DRAGONS!'

'Actually, I didn't slay it, and there was only one dragon,' Whetstone began modestly, massaging his throat.

'SAVIOUR OF THE MAGIC CUP!'

'Well, yes, I suppose—'

'DEFEATER OF THIEVES!'

'I'm not sure that—'

'FAVOURITE OF THE GODS!'

Whetstone tried not to grin as the Vikings of Krud started to stamp their feet and chant his name: 'Whet-stone, Whet-stone, WHET-STONE!'

'Don't forget that Odin, Chief of the Gods, decided Whetstone was officially a Hero and gave him a mighty quest!' the cup squeaked over the racket.

Whetstone made a grab for the cup, which jumped on to Awfulrick's other shoulder.

'Shut up! You can't tell *anyone* about that.' The boy looked around in a panic.

'The way you got rid of that dragon was brilliant!' cried a short, round Viking, wiping tears out of his eyes. 'Best thing to happen in Krud since Bjorn Brown Trousers was bitten on the bottom by a bear!'

The man from the longboat stroked his enormous beard. 'You sound like the sort of adventurous young man we could use on our crew.'

'YOU CAN'T HAVE HIM!' Awfulrick bellowed, squeezing Whetstone's shoulder in a move that was both comforting and a tiny bit suffocating. 'HE'S STAYING IN KRUD. HE'S OUR GOOD-LUCK CHARM.'

Whetstone winced.

The cup jumped off Awfulrick's shoulder and landed

in Whetstone's hands. It peered up at him with ruby eyes. 'Why won't you let me tell them how the adventure ends?' it complained. 'That was the best bit. You, me, Lotta, Odin, the riddle . . .'

Whetstone wiggled away from Awfulrick and wrapped his hands round the cup to muffle its voice. 'Shhh!'

The cup narrowed its eyes. 'But it was amazing! Odin ordered you—'

Whetstone tightened his hands round the cup's mouth, but odd words still escaped:

'Skera Harp—

Dwarves—

Loki—'

Thinking the cup had finished, Whetstone relaxed his hands.

'SAVE THE NINE WORLDS!' the cup squealed loudly.

The Vikings gave a massive cheer. Cups of ale were thrown into the air. The dogs dozing in front of the fire woke up and started barking. Arrows were shot into the rafters, knocking down dust, cobwebs and an unfortunate squirrel.

Whetstone slunk into a corner by the fireplace. 'You have to shut up! I *know* about the quest. I was there, remember? I have to return the cursed harp strings to the Dwarves before Loki finds them. But it's not exactly *easy*, is it?'

'No one ever said being a Hero was easy,' the cup replied tartly. 'Otherwise anyone could do it. Besides, I'm here to help you.'

'Yeah, thanks,' Whetstone grumbled.

'It's no use getting stroppy with me.' The cup pouted. 'I didn't steal the Skera Harp and curse your whole family. That was *mostly* Loki.'

'I *know*,' Whetstone hissed, squeezing the cup again. 'And *don't tell me* that Loki will be back, because I know that too. He's a shapeshifter, so being eaten by a dragon won't stop him for long.'

The cup snickered. 'He's just got to wait until the dragon poos him out!'

'Poo!' yelled a tufty-haired Viking, waving his mug in the air. Whetstone huddled deeper into the shadows.

'You do remember the riddle I gave you, don't you?' the cup asked, oblivious to Whetstone's discomfort. 'When I told you your fate?' The cup took a breath, and recited:

You will seek to find those who have been pulled apart,
A journey high and deep, into Yggdrasil's heart.

Whetstone gritted his teeth. The cup could tell the fortune of anyone who held it, and that was the reason Loki made Whetstone take it in the first place. It had told Whetstone that his fate was to reunite his family, but Loki knew that by finding his parents Whetstone would also reveal the location of the cursed harp strings, and Loki wanted the harp strings more than anything . . .

One you will find below, in an ice-locked land,
Still living but alone, for Hel holds him in her hand.

16

'That's enough,' Whetstone gave the cup a little shake. 'I remember. It's not exactly something you forget.'

The cup fell silent. Whetstone unpeeled his hands. He had been holding it so tightly the pattern from the cup's sides was imprinted on his palms.

'I don't know why you've been hanging around here,' the cup complained. 'The sooner you start looking, the sooner I can make up more fantastic poems about your valiant quest!'

'I've been busy planning stuff! The Nine Worlds are depending on me – it's a lot of pressure.' Whetstone sighed, his shoulders slumping. 'And I've been waiting for Lotta. She promised to come back and help me, but I haven't heard from her in weeks.'

'Of course not,' the cup replied. 'She's busy with Valkyrie business. You need to get on with things on your own. Have you figured out where the first harp string is yet?'

'It must be in Helheim – that's where Hel lives,' Whetstone muttered. 'But how do I get there? I can't even get out of Krud.'

'Not with that attitude,' the cup replied primly. 'Helheim is the Land of Lost Things. So you should, you know . . . get lost!' The cup jumped on to a nearby table and vanished among the Vikings.

Needing some fresh air, Whetstone sidled to the door of the Great Hall and slipped out. Dark clouds hung above him, filling the sky with the promise of yet more rain. Whetstone pushed his hood down, enjoying the novel sensation of being outside and dry at the same time.

His feet unthinkingly followed the familiar path towards

the field outside the village. He made this journey at least once a day, visiting a boy-sized boulder, which was all that was left of Loki's son, Vali. Loki had transformed him into a rock when Vali finally defied him. Although Whetstone and Vali had never been friends, Whetstone found it reassuring to visit what was left of him. It helped remind him that his adventures weren't some sort of mad dream.

Whetstone stuck his hands in his pockets, fingers feeling for the crumpled *Guide to the Nine Worlds*. It was the last thing Lotta had given him before returning to Asgard. Lotta had got in a lot of trouble for accidentally bringing Whetstone to the world of the Gods instead of a dead Hero like she was supposed to. It was only when Whetstone had proved his worth by getting rid of the dragon that she was able to continue with her Valkyrie training.

Whetstone pulled the tattered pages out of his pocket. Another fragment of paper was stuck to the front cover.

I'M SORRY - STUCK IN ASGARD.
DON'T START THE QUEST WITHOUT ME!
LOTTA

Lotta had sent him that note three weeks earlier. Since then, there had been nothing. *Don't start the quest without me.* It was all very well Lotta saying that, but he was the one left kicking his heels in Krud, waiting for her to show up. He couldn't exactly march up to Asgard and find her himself. He smiled, imagining the scene.

'Excuse me, Odin, Chief of the Gods, Spear Shaker, One-Eyed Thunderer, is Lotta the Valkyrie in? I need to talk to her.' Whetstone sniggered, picturing the God's expression.

Whetstone rounded the bend, following the path of churned mud to Vali's boulder. Sometimes when the light was right, you could almost see a face in the rock. Lotta had said that Vali had been transformed into a Troll, not just an ordinary boulder, and when the sun went down he would revert to his usual, horrible self and should be able to move. Except he hadn't moved an inch so far, so maybe he was just a boulder, after all.

Whetstone glanced up, expecting to see the familiar shape outlined against the horizon.

His feet stopped. His knees locked.

The boulder was gone.

Whetstone spun on the spot, his heart hammering. He was definitely in the right place – there was even a patch of dead grass where the boulder had stood. Vali had gone, but something had been left behind in his place, burned into the grass in tall black letters.

He'S ComINg

Chapter Two

Ankle-deep in Krud

As Whetstone stared in horror at the place where Vali's boulder should've been, a dark-skinned figure on horseback landed over by the Great Hall with a *thump, thump, THUMP, squish*. Thighbiter, the flying warhorse, whinnied and pulled his hoof out of the sucking mud.

'Don't be such a softy.' Lotta dropped the reins and pushed her helmet away from her eyes. 'We've just got to pick something up and then it's straight back to Asgard before anyone knows we've gone.'

Like all Valkyries, Lotta lived in Asgard, the Home of the Gods. Asgard sat at the top of the world tree, and its inhabitants ruled over the rest of the Nine Worlds. Valkyries were elite warriors whose main purpose was to help Odin build his ghostly army in readiness for Ragnarok, the final battle against the Frost Giants. They were *not* supposed to sneak out and make secret visits to the human world of Midgard below.

Lotta tucked the key to the gates of Asgard (which she had – ahem – *borrowed*) into her wrist guards and slid off the horse's back, landing ankle-deep in sludge. 'Yuck.'

Her horse snickered.

'I told you – I'm not going to muck it up. This is my chance to come back to Midgard for a bit – officially.'

The warhorse tossed his mane, showering the girl in raindrops.

'Hey! It wasn't my idea to have a stupid poetry contest.' Lotta wiped rain off her face. 'But the prize is to deliver a package to Njord, God of Coastal Waters, who just *happens* to live on Midgard. So, while we're doing that, we can take a little detour to see Whetstone and help him out with the quest.' She grinned.

Thighbiter looked unconvinced and flared his nostrils. Lotta patted him.

'It'll be fine. But you know what I'm like with remembering poems – I just need a little . . . help.'

The horse made a noise that sounded like a cross between a snort and a laugh.

'Everyone is probably in the Great Hall.' Lotta led Thighbiter towards the largest building in the village. She paused in the doorway to unhook her circular shield from the horse's saddle. The six sections glowed faintly, showing how strong her powers were in each key skill. She examined it. 'Do you think this trip counts as Collecting Fallen Warriors?'

The horse curled his lip.

'No, I don't think so either. I couldn't get hold of the invisibility gauntlets the trainee Valkyries usually use on our trips to Midgard, so I'll have to use some of the shield's power instead.'

She pulled the shield on to her arm and concentrated hard. The shield flickered and Lotta started to fade, her clothes and skin blending in with the background, chameleon-like.

'I only need to disappear enough so that the Vikings don't notice me.' Her voice was as indistinct as her appearance. 'I'll be super quick. Then it's back to Asgard before you can say *Odin the One-Eyed Eats Only Onions*.'

She pushed open the door, the splintery wood blurry but visible through her arm. A thick wave of steam poured out, accompanied by a boom of noise.

Large men sat in clusters on wooden benches; on one side of the room a woman sang a song no one was listening to, and in the corner two sweaty men arm wrestled while their friends cheered them on. Lotta immediately felt better: this was just like Valhalla. Only smaller and not as good, obviously. Under the mud and scars, all Vikings were the same, really: feasting and partying until their pasty faces turned red and they collapsed on the floor.

Lotta straightened her metal-and-leather breastplate, and crept forward.

She felt guilty that she hadn't made it back to Midgard to visit Whetstone earlier, but her teacher Scold seemed determined to keep her occupied. Just when Lotta thought she had scrubbed every table and polished all the boots in Valhalla, Scold would find more. It was almost like Scold was keeping her busy on purpose . . . but at least Lotta's Valkyrie scores were improving because of it.

Lotta sighed, realizing Whetstone was nowhere to be

seen. Maybe he had already left on the quest. No matter –
she would just have to catch up with him later. Her shield
gave a quiver and her outline started to grow more solid. Lotta
screwed up her face in concentration. She couldn't lose focus
now. She needed to find the cup and get back to Asgard, not
be distracted by scruffy boys who badly needed a bath. She
fixed her eyes on a gleam of gold by the fireplace, and crept
forward. Her shield trembled again. Lotta felt a prickle of
fear – the power was draining away far more quickly than she
had expected. She needed to get the cup and get out of there
before she reappeared completely.

A scream cut through the noise, making Lotta jump. Heart
beating wildly, she spun round. They couldn't be screaming at
her: she was still invisible – wasn't she? Her shield gave a final
shudder and Lotta fully rematerialized in the middle of the
Great Hall.

A teenage boy with red hair and a big nose pointed straight at her. 'It's that GIRL!'

Lotta reached for the sword strapped across her back. Heads and weapons turned towards her; she raised her fading shield.

'WAIT!' bellowed Awfulrick, shoving his way forward. 'I KNOW YOU! YOU'RE THAT VALKYRIE YOUNG WHETSTONE SAVED!'

'Excuse me?' Lotta lowered her shield. '*I* saved *him*, actually—'

'She's a Valkyrie? A real Valkyrie?' asked a man who smelt strongly of seawater and sweat.

Awfulrick nodded. 'I TOLD YOU YOUNG WHETSTONE WAS SOMETHING SPECIAL. HE EVEN HAS A VALKYRIE ASSISTANT.'

Lotta's brown eyes narrowed. '*What* did you just call me?'

Awfulrick took a step back at her expression.

'Are you here to take us to Valhalla?' called a hopeful voice.

'No.'

There was a disappointed chorus of 'Oo-ooohh'. Every Viking dreamed of one day going to Valhalla – it was their paradise.

Lotta slid her sword back into its scabbard. 'Where is Whetstone, anyway?'

'Probably off sulking somewhere,' said the large-nosed youth who had screamed at her.

'So he *is* still in Krud.' Lotta grinned. 'Could you pass on a message for me? I've got a plan to . . . come . . . back . . .'

24

Lotta slowed as she looked at the Vikings crowding around her. 'Are there more people in Krud now? And why does it smell like fish?'

'WE'VE GOT SOME VISITORS.' Awfulrick pointed at the group of damp-looking men. 'THEIR BOAT WASHED UP ON THE BEACH!'

'But we're leaving again tomorrow,' a man with a large scar running down his face explained.

Lotta nodded slowly. Everyone was staring at her. She was uncomfortably reminded of the time she had forgotten the words to the Ballad of Bjork the Boring, and everyone in Valhalla had stopped quaffing their drinks to watch. Lotta squashed the memory and straightened her shoulders. 'I'm here because I need to borrow something.'

'You can have my sword,' called a thin-faced man. 'If I can go to Valhalla afterwards.'

'No – take mine!' called someone else.

Before Lotta could blink, she was surrounded by pointed weapons. A long sword threatened to slice off one of her black curls. She pushed the blade away. 'I don't need anyone's sword. I need –' she pointed a finger past Awfulrick's shoulder – 'the cup.'

Everyone swivelled to look as the golden cup twitched and spun, enjoying the attention.

Bragi crossed his arms. 'You can't just barge in here and take our magic cup!'

'BE QUIET, BRAGI,' yelled Awfulrick. 'SHE'S A VALKYRIE – SHE CAN HAVE WHATEVER SHE LIKES.'

25

A sharp-faced woman raised her hand. 'What do you want it for? Are you going on an adventure?'

The cup jumped off its shelf and landed with a clang on the table nearest Lotta. 'The mighty quest as decreed by Odin begins! I knew you couldn't do it without me.'

'What quest?' asked Bragi. 'The weasel never said anything about a quest.'

Lotta waved her hands; if Whetstone hadn't told the Vikings about his quest, he must've had a good reason. She wondered if he'd got any further in puzzling out the clues in the riddle. 'Never mind that – I need it to win a poetry contest.'

'POETRY!' the cup squeaked. 'That's my favourite thing!'

Bragi snorted.

Lotta gave him a LOOK. A Category Three Valkyrie Death Stare, to be exact. Bragi turned pale as his backbone melted in response.

VALKYRIE DEATH STARES

Category 1
Mild annoyance. Response: Subject may start to apologize.

Category 2
Irritation. Response: Subject may start to whimper; loss of
    speech is to be expected.

Category 3
Anger. Response: Subject may start backing away; cut off
    escape routes.

Category 4
Rage. Response: Subject may wet themselves; stand well back
    to avoid splashes.

Category 5
Fury. Response: Call a doctor. Order a coffin. It's all over.

The sharp-faced woman called out again. 'Do you need
someone to carry it? I'll come to Asgard with you!'

'No.' Lotta scooped up the cup. 'I'll bring it back as soon
as I can.'

The cup squeaked in excitement as Lotta kicked the door
open and ducked into the rainy night. 'Asgard, here we come!'

Chapter Three

The most Epic-est Poetry Ever

From the outside, Valhalla looked like an overgrown version of a normal Viking Great Hall, albeit one with walls made of ranks of shields and with a roof thatched with spears. It towered imposingly over the other buildings in Asgard. Lotta huddled in the doorway, clutching the cup.

'So, you understand the plan?'

The cup hopped up on to her shoulder. 'Asgard!' It jiggled up and down in excitement. 'I haven't been here in YEARS!'

Lotta grabbed at it. 'Oh, that's right – you used to belong to Frigg, and that's how you got your magical powers. How did you end up in Krud?'

The cup stopped jiggling. 'Never mind that,' it muttered. 'Some people can't take a joke – that's all.'

'I don't need jokes. I need Epic Poetry. The most Epic-ist Epic Poetry Asgard has ever heard.' Lotta adjusted the scabbard holding her sword across her back. 'You hide here until it's my turn – then you tell me what to say and I say it.' She popped the cup on top of her scabbard, next to the sword. 'It's perfect. We can't fail!'

Lotta slipped into the enormous hall. Inside, the walls seemed to stretch for miles. The ceiling was somewhere far, far up above, hidden by smoke and shadows. Tables the size of boats filled the space, each one crowded with great fighters plucked from battle sites by the Valkyries. She swiftly joined the other Valkyries busily shoving benches and tables out of the way, sometimes with warriors still sitting on them.

Lotta was currently the lowest class of Valkyrie, a Class Three. In order to move up to Class Two (and then on to Class One), she needed to score at least sixty per cent in each of the six key skills, which were recorded on their glowing shields.

Valkyrie Training School Report

Name: Brings-A-Lot-Of-Scrapes-And-Grazes (Lotta)
Class: Third

Skill		Previous score
Fighting:	40%	(35%)
Horse Riding:	42%	(30%)
Epic Poetry:	30%	(28%)
Transforming into Swans:	51%	(38%)
Serving Mead in Valhalla:	57%	(53%)
Collecting Fallen Warriors:	59.9%	(0%)
Overall Hero Score:	47%	(31%)

A surprising improvement – don't disappoint me again.

Signed: *Blood-Runs-Cold*, Leader of the Valkyries

Class Twos had much more exciting jobs than Class Threes, like delivering prophecies or appearing in visions while screaming and waving spears. Lotta couldn't wait.

'All right, Class Threes!' A large woman in a spiky breastplate waved her arms. 'Gather round.'

This was Scold, short for Blood-Runs-Cold. Like all Valkyries, she had a name that made strong men quiver and weak men run screaming for their mummies. None of them would admit it, but she had the same effect on the trainee Valkyries. She was a tall olive-skinned woman with glossy black hair and a booming voice, which she mostly used for telling the trainees off VERY LOUDLY. 'You are each to perform ONE POEM. You can choose the topic of your poem from War, Fighting, Combat or Biscuits.'

The trainees looked at each other in confusion.

A girl with two long silver plaits and ivory skin raised her eyebrows. 'Biscuits?'

'Yes, biscuits. Glinting-Fire suggested it.'

Across the room, Glinting-Fire looked up from her clipboard. She was a short Class One Valkyrie from the far north, with bright eyes and *tupik* tattoos across her tanned face and hands. Lotta shuffled sideways so that she was hidden behind another trainee. Glinting-Fire had a fearsome reputation. Her most-hated habit was springing surprise quizzes on the trainees, determined to weed out anyone who didn't know their Heroes from their elbows.

The trainees exploded into whispers.

'I heard Glinting-Fire tried to take over from Scold, but Odin wouldn't let her,' one muttered.

'I heard she wanted to put us all in boot camps and do twenty-four-hour training,' said another.

'I heard she sleeps on a bed of spikes to keep her tough.'

'I heard she does a thousand push-ups every morning and she can fly!'

'Huh. She's only here because Lotta messed up – I don't see why we should all suffer.'

Lotta stared down at her boots. Although never exactly popular, Lotta had reached new lows since her adventures with Whetstone. Many of the Valkyries, especially Glinting-Fire, thought Lotta a troublemaker who had disgraced them all by breaking the rules and wondered if Odin had been right to let her back into Asgard.

'Ahem.' Scold glared the trainees into silence. 'Odin, Frigg and Freyja will be here shortly to judge the contest.'

The girl with long silver plaits put her hand in the air. 'Doesn't Loki normally judge the poetry stuff?'

'Loki is busy, Flee.'

Lotta tried not to smirk. She had been there when Loki was eaten by the dragon; he was probably still stuck somewhere inside its bum.

An identical girl but with one long plait and one silver tuft sniffed. This was Flay, Flee's twin sister. Flay still blamed Lotta for her lopsided haircut, even thought it had been her own fault, really. It was also the twins' own fault that they had been caught and punished for helping Loki in his search for the magic cup. But this didn't seem to matter. The twins hated Lotta more than ever, especially since Lotta's Valkyrie scores had started to improve and she was making them look bad in comparison. Lotta gave Flay a smug smile, just to annoy her.

'I suggest that you spend the next few minutes thinking about which poem you might chose to recite,' Scold continued, ignoring the twins. 'Remember, VICTORY and SPLENDOUR to the winner – SHAME and LOSS to the losers.'

Flee sniggered. 'Yeah, a-Lotta loss.'

Flay stifled a giggle. Lotta stopped smiling.

The girls fanned out, each trying to think of the best war, fighting or combat poem. Lotta slunk away, keenly aware that Glinting-Fire was watching her. She straightened her hairy socks and tried to speak without moving her lips.

'So, what've you got?'

The cup peeped out of Lotta's scabbard. 'Is that Glinting-Fire?'

'The one with the clipboard? Yup.'

'She's looking at you like she hates you.'

'She hates everyone.'

'No, really – she's giving you a proper glare. Is that a

32

Category Four? How's your bladder?'

Lotta's response was lost in a sudden roar from the warriors of Valhalla. Odin and Frigg had arrived. The trainees shuffled into a line as a tall, tanned man in a blue cloak moved through the crowd. He had a long beard and one eye was covered with a patch. Two ravens swooped through the hall. They were Odin's helpers and brought him news from across the Nine Worlds. One landed on a table and pecked hopefully at some pickled onions.

Frigg, the Goddess of Family, walked with long strides, her skirts flashing green and blue in the candlelight. Her honey-blonde hair twisted into a thick plait supporting a curved headdress. Together they joined Glinting-Fire in the space in front of the Class Three Valkyries. Glinting-Fire said something to Odin, who laughed. Lotta's hands went slippery with sweat.

Silence fell as a third figure entered.

'All right, Freyja?' called a hopeful voice from the back.

Frigg rolled her eyes.

The Goddess of Love and Sorcery tossed her black twists and swept through the room, a cloud of cat hair following her. Lotta fought down a sneeze. A gold necklace flashed against the brown skin of Freyja's throat, and multicoloured gems decorated the many rings on her fingers. 'Let's get on with it, shall we?'

The judges took their seats. Freyja produced a kitten from out of a pocket and placed it on her lap. Lotta's eyes started to sting. The other trainees shuffled nervously, but the kitten didn't seem to be making anyone else itchy. Lotta wiped her nose. Typical – just another way in which she was the odd one out.

Scold marched into the centre of the space and held out her hands for silence. Gradually the hall quietened. A dish clattered to the floor from somewhere in the back.

'Sorry!' called out a small voice.

'Gods, Goddesses, warriors and Valkyries!' Scold began, her voice echoing around the enormous hall. 'Welcome to the

Annual Asgardian Poetry Contest!'

There was a groan from the collected warriors. Someone muttered, 'I hate poetry.' Scold glared.

'Sorry.'

'As I was saying –' Scold continued to glare at the poetry hater – 'we are going to have a POETRY contest and the winner will get the opportunity to serve Odin by delivering a package. So, no talking. Understand?'

The warriors muttered and shuffled their feet.

'I said: UNDERSTAND?'

There was a reluctant chorus of, 'Yes, Scold.'

'Let the contest BEGIN!'

❀

'So he crushed his enemy's head between his mighty elbows –'

The trainee droned on, her skin tawny-brown in the candlelight. Lotta was sure several lifetimes had passed since she'd started speaking.

'– and the puddles of blood and goo, which dripped –'

Flay was openly snoring. It shouldn't be possible for war poetry to be THIS dull.

'– ravens, and slugs, and badgers, and other animals came to feast –'

Flee poked her sister awake as Scold stepped forward.

'Yes, thank you. I think we've heard enough.'

The girl slunk off to find a seat. Freyja looked relieved. Odin smiled.

Most of the trainees had already presented their poems. Only Flee and Lotta were left. Flee sat straight up, radiating keenness. Lotta chewed her thumbnail worriedly. She was sure the cup would come up with *something* . . .

Scold turned back to the group. 'Enemies-Flee-Before-Me, let's hear what you've got.'

Flee stood up self-importantly and strode into the centre of the circle, stomping on Lotta's toe on the way. 'I would like to present, *The Saga of Wiggo the Wild*!'

Odin leaned forward; even the warriors looked interested. Lotta groaned inwardly. *Wiggo the Wild* was a really good poem. If Flee got all the way through, she would be hard to beat.

Flee took a deep breath. Her chest puffed out so far that her feet almost lifted off the floor. '*LISTEN!*' Several bats fell from the rafters.

To the Saga I now tell.
There was once a Man named Wiggo,
Who had the most enormous Collection of Cabbages!

Flee stalked up and down, gesturing wildly. Lotta slumped in her chair; there was no way she could beat this.

And so Wiggo did Hack at the Intruders,
'I will use their Bones to support my Peas and Beans,
Their ruined Armour to build Scarecrows,
And their Tears to Water my Cabbages!'

. . .

Flee jumped on to a table for her big finish, her arms raised high in the air.

Never will they Gaze upon another Cauliflower.
Thus ends the Saga of—

From the side of the hall Glinting-Fire gave a meaningful cough. Flee scrunched up her face as if in pain and proclaimed: '*WEIRDO the MILD!*'

A giggle came from the back of the room.

'Did she just say *Weirdo the Mild*?' Akrid, a Class Two Valkyrie with long dreadlocks, whispered.

Flee dropped her arms, her pale face turning bright red. Although whether this was from embarrassment or the effort of screaming for the last twenty minutes, Lotta couldn't be sure. One of the tables of warriors burst into laughter. Flay hid her face in her hands. Lotta pushed down a giggle, trying to disguise it with a cough.

'Amateurs,' the cup huffed.

Flee stamped her foot. 'I said Milbo the Filed! No, Filbo the Piled! No—'

Raising her hands for silence, Scold stepped forward. Glinting-Fire smiled to herself and ticked something off on her clipboard. After a few moments everyone quietened down.

'Thank you, Flee,' Scold said as Flee slunk back to her seat. Her face blazing. 'That was . . . unusual.'

Someone at the back barked a laugh and was quickly shushed.

'Now for our final competitor, Brings-A-Lot-Of-Scrapes-And-Grazes!'

There was a murmur from the warriors in the audience. As well as upsetting the Valkyries, Lotta's adventures with Whetstone had not gone down well in Valhalla. The Heroes and warriors were very touchy about who was allowed to join them and, even though Odin had said he was a Hero, Whetstone's craftiness made them uncomfortable.

Lotta squared her shoulders and stepped forward.

'Just repeat exactly what I say,' the cup muttered into Lotta's ear.

Lotta swallowed her nerves and nodded. Flee and Flay peered at her. If Lotta hadn't heard Flee just make a big mistake, she would've thought they looked – smug?

'I would like to present,' the cup prompted.

'*I would like to present*,' Lotta recited woodenly, fixing her eyes on Odin's left ear to control her nerves, her mouth dry.

'A riddle.'

'*A riddle.*'

Frigg leaned forward. 'Is that allowed?' she asked her fellow judges. 'This is supposed to be a poetry contest.'

'A riddle means it will be over quicker,' Freyja replied, stroking the kitten.

'In that case, yes, it is allowed,' Frigg announced quickly. 'This chair really is uncomfortable. Proceed, Brings-A-Lot-Of-Scrapes-And-Grazes.'

Lotta gulped and crossed her fingers.

'*I am round, but I am not a wheel . . .*' the cup began.

Lotta echoed it word for word.

I am made of flour, but I do not grow.
I am hard, but I crumble in water.
You can hold me and my brothers in your hand.
What am I?

Frigg glanced at Odin, who wrinkled his forehead in thought. The warriors around them screwed up their faces. They were in Valhalla for their fighting skills, not their thinking ones. Odin's ravens took off, searching the hall for clues.

Akrid, the Class Two, furrowed her brow in concentration. What was the answer to the riddle? Did anyone know?

'This is ridiculous!' Flee snorted. 'Brings-A-Lot-Of-Snots-And-Bogeys cannot have come up with a riddle we cannot answer.'

'Oh, I get it!' said her sister, smiling. 'The answer is—'

Flee elbowed her savagely in the ribs.

After a few moments, Odin leaned forward. 'I think you have us stumped,' he said, his low voice causing a plate to vibrate off the end of the table. 'What is the answer?'

Lotta grinned, her shoulders sagging in relief. 'It's a biscuit.'

The muttering intensified.

'But a biscuit isn't round like a whee— Oh!' Akrid began.

Glinting-Fire tutted.

'Wonderful!' cried Odin, striding forward to shake Lotta by the hand. The girl's whole arm was yanked up and down. 'I shall have to remember that one.'

39

Jiggling around inside Lotta's scabbard, the cup squeaked with excitement.

'I think your Epic Poetry score might have just gone up a bit,' Scold said, crossing her arms and trying not to smile. 'Glinting-Fire has prepared the parcel. You're to take it straight to Njord in Midgard. And – please – don't bring anything back with you this time.'

As Lotta was grudgingly congratulated by the other Valkyries, Flee and Flay skulked in the shadows.

'Well done, girls.' Glinting-Fire approached them, scribbling something on her clipboard. 'Phase One is nearly complete.'

'Yeah, no thanks to big mouth,' Flee sniffed. 'I didn't just humiliate myself in front of all of Valhalla for you to solve Lotta's riddle.'

'At least I *knew* the answer,' Flay retorted.

'That's enough,' Glinting-Fire snapped. 'The important thing is that Lotta won the contest.'

Flay tipped her head. 'But how could you be sure Lotta would win? She's usually rubbish at poetry.'

Glinting-Fire's lips went as tight and wrinkly as a cat's bum. 'She's been corrupted by the humans. I knew she couldn't resist cheating. She stole the magic cup.'

Flee raised her eyebrows in surprise.

'That mangy cup knows more poems about biscuits than you can shake a stick at. It's why it got kicked out of Asgard. It's supposed to tell people their fate, but it wouldn't stop reciting biscuit recipes: *two handfuls of oats, four spoonfuls*

40

of honey, a scoop of crushed ant eggs—'

'Yuck!' Flee screwed up her face.

'Exactly. That last one gave Frigg a dodgy tummy, and she loves biscuits. But the cup plus biscuits equals a win for Lotta.' Glinting-Fire smirked. 'Now Lotta is off to Midgard, and you two know what to do.'

Flay looked at her sister and grinned. 'Leave it to us. If Lotta likes Midgard so much, we'll see that she stays there.'

Chapter Four

A World of Adventure

As the sky lightened and the birds started to sing, Whetstone wrapped himself in his cloak and crept away from his hiding place. His face pale and eyes heavy, he had spent a restless night fretting about Vali's message: *He's coming.* There was only one person that could mean – Loki. Whetstone couldn't wait for Lotta any longer; he had to get out of Krud *now*. Even Vali had left, and he was made of rock!

Whetstone followed the narrow path down the cliffs towards the beach. The longboat lay peacefully on the shingle, its sail the only moving thing in the early morning breeze. Boats looked so calm – when they were on the shore. His stomach churned at the thought of bouncing through the waves on one.

Whetstone reached out to touch the curved wood. One way or another, he was going to get on that boat and leave Krud today. Then, when he was safely away from Loki, he could concentrate on finding his way to Helheim. Somehow.

A dark shadow loomed round the carved figurehead. Whetstone almost screamed in surprise, expecting Loki's twisted smile and scarred face to appear out of the sea mist. Instead, he was confronted by an enormous glossy ginger beard. Whetstone almost collapsed in relief.

The longboat man stroked his thick beard and regarded Whetstone carefully. 'A young man like you doesn't want to be cooped up in a place like Krud.'

'Don't I?' asked Whetstone weakly. He tried not to stare at the beard; it really was spectacular.

'No! You want to be out seeking Fortune and Glory in a World of Adventure! Don't you want everyone to know your name?'

A shiver shot down Whetstone's spine: once that had been all he'd wanted, and it was how Loki had manipulated him into stealing the cup. He peered suspiciously at the man. Loki was very fond of disguises, after all . . .

'Join our crew and you can visit places you've only dreamed about.'

'Oh yeah, like where?' Whetstone tilted his head, trying to see if the beard was held on with string.

The beard smiled conspiratorially. A gold tooth appeared. 'To the edges of Midgard and beyond.'

Whetstone's eyebrows shot up. 'You're trying to leave Midgard? Why?'

'Muspell, Niflheim and Helheim.' The man rubbed his freckled hands together. 'Imagine the adventures we could have in the Lower Worlds.'

Whetstone's heart thumped loudly – this was better than he had hoped. If the longboat crew knew how to reach Helheim, he could be on his way to finding the first harp string in no time! He licked his dry lips; he didn't want to appear to be too keen. 'But you can't. You can't go to Helheim – only the Gods can travel between worlds.'

'Is that so?' The man winked. He leaned in closer. 'There are weak points in every world. If you push through in just the right place, you find yourself somewhere else.'

'Where?'

'I happen to know a point that will lead us straight to the Land of Lost Things.' The man tapped the side of his nose. 'Ever lost something you wish you could find again, kid? It's all there, held by the Queen of the Dead.'

Whetstone gulped.

'Our names will go down in history.' The beard slapped Whetstone on the back. 'What glory is there in exploring Midgard? Everyone's been there. No – we're going to be the crew who visited Hel and came back again. I can hear the stories now.'

Whetstone's fingers twitched in excitement. So much for waiting for Lotta! He could join the longboat and have a whole crew of Vikings to help him in Helheim! Relief washed over Whetstone. It wasn't that he didn't want to complete the quest and be the Hero everyone thought he was, just that – well – it was the Land of the Dead. Who wanted to go there alone?

'So what do you say? Fancy joining our Happy Band of Explorers, or is there something better waiting for you here?'

Whetstone stilled, thinking of Vali's warning. He was pretty sure this man wasn't Loki, and even if the longboat crew turned out to be as mad as a box of frogs, he would at least be out of Krud. 'Awfulrick won't let me leave easily, not when I'm his "Good-luck Charm".'

The man attached to the beard held out a freckled hand. It was long-fingered and oddly slender. 'I'm Ulf,' he said as Whetstone shook his hand. 'And don't worry –' the beard twitched into a smile – 'I can get you out. No problem.'

❧

'WHERE'S THAT BOY GONE NOW!' Awfulrick bellowed a couple of hours later as the sun rose higher in the sky. 'HE'D BETTER NOT BE SNEAKING OFF AGAIN.'

Whetstone wiggled his shoulders. He had spent the morning dozing uncomfortably inside Ulf's cramped sea chest on the beach next to the longboat. Raindrops hammered on the lid and trickled in through the cracks, filling the small space with the scent of damp clothes and unwashed boy.

'WHETSTONE!'

The boy instinctively ducked his head.

'I'VE GOT A MESSAGE FOR YOU FROM THAT VALKYRIE GIRL!'

Whetstone shook his head. That was impossible. He would've known if Lotta had come to Krud. It was obviously a sneaky trick to lure him out. Anyway, he didn't need Lotta; he had Ulf now.

Whetstone bit back a yelp as the box was suddenly lifted into the air and tossed on the longboat's deck. Next came the crunch of shingle. Men's voices, shouting and cursing, surrounded him. With a wobble, the sea took hold of the boat. Whetstone closed his eyes and gulped, trying to ignore the rocking as the longboat men climbed aboard.

'Goodbye, Krud, and thanks for everything!' Ulf the Bearded yelled, thumping his fist on top of Whetstone's box, making him wince.

Then there was nothing but a rhythmic creaking and the splash of oars. Salt filled the air. Seagulls screamed overhead. Whetstone closed his eyes and resisted the urge to throw up on his boots. Being a Hero could be really rubbish sometimes.

Time passed slowly in the box. How long had he been in there? Hours? Days? Whetstone was just wondering if he should knock when the chest's lid opened, leaving the boy blinking in the sunlight. Above him waved the sail with the dark sea serpent on it, now repaired. Whetstone wheezed as a wave of seasickness washed over him.

'It's a stowaway!'

Whetstone peered out of the chest only to see Bragi. He was holding an oar. Whetstone groaned.

'He's not a stowaway.' Ulf grinned through his wobbly beard. 'And he's *our* good-luck charm now.'

The boat gave a sudden lurch – so did Whetstone's stomach. He hiccupped.

'That's it, kid. Breathe in that salty air. You don't get air like that in Krud.'

Whetstone climbed out of the chest on legs like jelly.

'I can't believe this,' Bragi snapped. 'Just when I thought

I was getting away from you.' He poked Whetstone with his oar. 'Don't get in my way – you're not the only one who can have adventures, you know.'

Whetstone opened his mouth to reply, but then closed it quickly. If words came out, so might . . . something else. Instead, he gripped the side of the boat and watched Krud vanish over the horizon.

A wooden bucket smacked Whetstone on the shoulder. He twisted round to see a man whose face reminded Whetstone of a lump of gristle. A long scar ran down one cheek, narrowly missing his eye.

'Oi, stowaway,' the man called. 'You have to earn your passage like the rest of us. There's water in the bottom. Start bailing.'

Bragi snorted a laugh.

Rubbing his shoulder, Whetstone picked up the bucket. He made his way to the stern of the boat, where a few inches of water had collected. He tried to balance one foot on either side of the puddle to keep his boots dry, but water splashed him in the face instead. The scarred man laughed as Whetstone wiped his face with his sleeve. Resentment bubbled inside him.

He wouldn't have to do this if Lotta had come back to help like she'd promised. She could travel between worlds; they could've gone straight to Helheim if she'd brought her flying horse.

Whetstone stooped down again, but before he could dip the bucket in the water, he was thrown sideways. The ship bucked and thrashed in suddenly churning waves.

The scarred man turned pale, which made his scar look even worse. He dropped his steering oar. 'He's coming!'

The other Vikings scrambled to grab weapons, shouting and shoving.

A shiver ran down Whetstone's spine. Who was coming? Loki couldn't be all the way out here, could he?

Sinuous grey-green coils thicker than a tree, maybe even thicker than a house, appeared in the water. Huge waves smacked into the boat, nearly capsizing it. One of the Vikings started to pray. A gigantic head – half lizard, half bull – rose out of the ocean. Four seaweed-stained horns decorated its head, and yellow-stained teeth poked out of its cave-like mouth. Water poured down on to the boat below.

Whetstone swallowed, unable to tear his eyes away from the monster. 'Loki? Is that you?'

'No – it's his son, Jormungandr, the Midgard Serpent!' yelled Ulf, brandishing his axe.

'What's he doing so close to shore?' Bragi spluttered. 'We couldn't have travelled that far from Krud.'

Jormungandr was a sea serpent supposedly so large he could encircle all of Midgard and still hold his tail in his mouth. He had been cast into the sea by Odin and now resided in the deepest parts of the ocean, rising only to eat the occasional ship, or whale. The longboat crew gaped at the monster before them. There was the sound of someone throwing up.

A dark tongue flicked out of the monster's mouth, tasting the air. Whetstone stood hypnotized – that sea monster was Loki's son? And he had thought Vali was weird. Loki must've sent Jormungandr to make sure Whetstone didn't leave Krud by sea. Whetstone shivered with fear, wondering who else Loki had helping him.

The serpent writhed, churning the water and pitching the boat from side to side. Men crashed together. Whetstone skidded towards the mast. He gripped on tightly to avoid being thrown overboard.

'I don't know what's happening,' Bragi called as he was almost squashed by a Viking in yellow trousers, 'but I can guarantee this is all Whetstone's fault.'

'Didn't they warn you about deadly sea monsters when you

joined up?' Whetstone yelled back. 'I thought you wanted an adventure?'

Jormungandr wrapped his sinewy body round the longboat and began to squeeze. Wood splintered as planks broke apart. Whetstone hugged the mast tightly and closed his eyes.

'Dear Odin,' he prayed. 'I could really use your help right now . . .'

Suddenly there was a crash of thunder and a blinding white light. The sea serpent shrieked and let go of the boat, which rocked back and forth sickeningly in the waves, as the Vikings were tossed about like bubbles in a cooking pot.

Four hooves hit the deck – *thud, thud, CRUNCH, SPLASH!* – followed by a horsey whinny. Whetstone disentangled himself from a collection of oars and looked straight at a metal-studded boot with flint toe caps, topped with a wrinkly sock.

'Lotta!'

The figure on horseback pulled off her helmet. She smoothed back her black curls. 'Whetstone? What are you doing here?'

Whetstone struggled to his feet. 'How—?'

Lotta held out a hand to silence him. She swung a leg over Thighbiter's saddle. 'I can't talk now – I'm on Valkyrie business.'

'But—?' Whetstone gestured to where the sea serpent had been a moment before. The sea was now eerily calm, Jormungandr having sunk back beneath the waves. The Viking crew hustled towards the prow of the boat. There seemed to be a fight going on as to who could stand the furthest away. One man even clung to the snarling dragon figurehead.

Lotta puffed her chest out and put her hands on her hips. 'It's all right,' she called to them. 'I know visitors from Asgard are scary, but I'm not going to hurt you.'

'I don't think it's you –' Whetstone began.

Lotta turned back to Whetstone, her face scrunched up. 'I appreciate you making the effort to come out here, but why didn't you wait for me in Krud? I gave Awfulrick a message yesterday to say I was coming.'

Whetstone's mouth opened and closed noiselessly.

Lotta gave him poke. 'Good to see you've been keeping yourself out of trouble, anyway.'

Despite his shock, Whetstone couldn't help but laugh. Some of the tension left his shoulders. He knew he should be annoyed with Lotta for not helping him sooner, but he was just too relieved to see her.

Ulf stepped forward. 'Now look here, young lady—'

Lotta ignored him. 'How did you know this was where I was supposed to deliver the package?' Lotta unstrapped a wooden box from behind her saddle. It rocked and hissed as though whatever was inside was desperate to escape. Ulf stepped back again.

'I didn't. I was just trying to get out of Krud.' The box shuddered. Whetstone peered at it curiously. 'What is in there?'

'It's a gift for Njord, God of Coastal Waters.' Lotta lifted the lid a crack – a furious brown paw poked out, trying to claw anything it could reach.

'It's a cat?'

'Not just any cat. It's for Njord to pass on to his wife, Skadi. They've had another row. *Achoo!*' Lotta wiped her nose on her wrist guard. Whetstone's forehead wrinkled in confusion.

'It's one of Freyja's cats. You know, the Goddess of Love?' Lotta sighed. 'She's mad about cats. That's why brides get them as wedding presents.'

'So it's a special *love-cat*?'

Lotta nodded.

Whetstone tried to keep up. 'You've come all the way out here to deliver a love-cat to the God of Coastal Waters?'

'Uh huh.'

Whetstone tore his eyes away from the box and peered out over the quiet ocean. 'Well, the good news is: Jormungandr doesn't seem to like cats.'

'Jormungandr? Why are you messing about with him?' Lotta wiped her nose again. Thighbiter snickered. 'Hold this, will you?' Lotta plopped the yowling box into Bragi's arms. She looked around expectantly. 'Well, where is he?'

'Jormungandr?' asked Bragi. 'He's in the water.'

'No.' Lotta snorted. 'Njord. He's supposed to meet me

here. This is definitely where Glinting-Fire told me to come, and she never gets stuff like this wrong.'

Whetstone and Bragi looked at each other in confusion.

'We haven't seen him.' Whetstone explained. 'Unless he's disguised as a sea serpent.'

'He must be late.' Lotta tutted. 'Typical.'

Bragi held the yowling box away from him. 'This thing stinks.'

A strong breeze blew from the north, bringing with it a distinctly cheesy aroma. It rustled the ends of Whetstone's hair and made goosebumps rise on his arms. 'I don't think that's the cat,' he said. 'Can anyone else smell . . . feet?'

The Vikings turned to each other.

The scarred man tutted. 'I told you lot to change your socks before we left Krud.'

Ulf shaded his eyes to look out to sea. 'There!' He pointed towards the northern horizon, his beard glinting in the sunlight. 'It's a boat.' The rest of the Vikings crowded round him to see.

Thighbiter stamped his hooves, making the damaged deck wobble. Lotta's shield, strapped behind his saddle, gave a flicker. Lotta patted the horse's neck. 'It must be Njord coming to collect his cat.'

'But why does it smell of feet?' asked Bragi, trying to keep hold of the thrashing box.

The boat drew closer, black sails rippling in the breeze. The sea bubbled and churned.

'There goes Jormungandr,' Whetstone called as the sea

monster rose from the ocean, water pouring off his head, seaweed dangling fetchingly from one horn.

Lotta gaped. 'I thought you were joking about him!' She nudged Whetstone. 'You'd better do something, or that ship is finished.'

'Why me?!'

'Because you're a Hero!'

Whetstone swallowed. 'Yeah, of course.' He turned to Ulf. 'Have we got a really big net or anything?'

Ulf said nothing, just crossing his arms.

'Really helpful,' Whetstone muttered.

As the Viking crew watched, the monster twisted his long body to encircle the boat. Whetstone held his breath. But instead of crushing the ship, Jormungandr swam round it like a massive scaly dog chasing its own tail.

A heavy weight settled in Whetstone's stomach. 'That isn't Njord, is it?'

Lotta shook her head.

'And Jormungandr isn't attacking it?'

Lotta bit her lip, her brown eyes fixed on approaching ship.

'Because his dad is sailing it?'

Lotta nodded.

Loki.

Whetstone closed his eyes, his stomach feeling as though it were full of rocks.

'Naglfar,' Lotta breathed. 'The ship made of dead men's toenails.'

'Toenails? That's disgusting,' spluttered Bragi.

'I thought Loki was still inside the dragon.' Lotta reached for her sword. 'He never came back to Asgard.'

Whetstone opened his eyes again, suddenly remembering why he was stuck on this boat in the first place. 'You would know,' he said sourly.

Lotta stared at him. 'What's that supposed to mean? I got this job specially so I could have an excuse to come back to Midgard and help you. Now I'm wondering why I bothered.'

'It's getting closer.' Bragi dumped the yowling box on to the deck and reached for his own sword. 'How many people can your horse carry?'

Thighbiter tried to take a bite out of his hair.

'Maybe Loki's not on it?' Whetstone said, twisting his cloak between his fingers as the smelly boat grew closer. A kernel of hope grew in his chest. 'Maybe it came loose from its moorings completely innocently, and it's just a coincidence that it's here, miles out to sea in the same random place that we are?'

Lotta raised her eyebrows.

Whetstone glanced at her. 'No, I don't believe it either.'

The sails snapped in the breeze as the ship drew closer, Jormungandr nipping playfully at its prow. Whetstone looked around for a weapon. Unusually for a Viking, he wasn't much of a fighter, preferring to run and hide rather than face Death or Glory in hand-to-hand combat. He picked up an oar. At his feet, the cat thrashed about inside its box. Thighbiter tossed his mane.

'It's coming right for us!' yelled the scarred man.

Ulf strode to the prow and waved his hands above his head. 'Stop! I did what you asked. We have the boy! STOP!'

Whetstone's mouth fell open. Lotta pivoted to stare at Ulf.

'I *said* this was your fault!' Bragi spat.

Ulf turned to face them. He slowly reached up and tugged on one corner of his ferocious beard. It peeled away with a faint sucking noise, revealing a fresh-faced young woman underneath. Bragi's jaw hung open, making him look a bit like a haddock.

'I knew it was a fake beard!' Whetstone cried as a burly crew member grabbed the back of his tunic, lifting Whetstone up on to his tiptoes. Lotta rolled her eyes as a second crewman grabbed her arms.

Ulf carefully tucked the beard into her tunic. 'I am Snotra the Cutthroat,' she announced. 'And I've made a deal with Loki.'

Chapter Five

Toenails and Fish Scales

Whetstone and Bragi stared at the figure in front of them. Without the disguise, Snotra was a sharp-faced young woman with a topknot of strawberry-blonde hair, one gold tooth and, Whetstone noted with a lump in his throat, a very determined expression.

'But you said we were going on an adventure!' Bragi spluttered.

Snotra crossed her arms. 'We are. Well, I am.'

Whetstone fixed his eyes on Snotra; the oar slipped from his hands. The cloth of his tunic pulled tight across his neck.

Snotra paced towards him. 'I needed a way to get you on the boat.' Her thin eyebrows lowered into two sharp lines on her face. 'You must've seen my message back in Krud? *He's coming!*' She waggled her fingers at them. 'Whooo! Scary!'

'That was *you*?' Whetstone wobbled on his tiptoes.

'Yes – and you should be grateful. Without my little push, you would still be stuck there.' Snotra turned to face the northern horizon. 'Loki promised me safe passage to the Lower Worlds in exchange for –' she waved dismissively at

58

Whetstone – 'you.' The toenail boat loomed over her shoulder. 'I just had to bring you *here*.'

'Loki *arranged* for *you* to be here – Glinting-Fire *sent me* here,' Lotta mumbled to herself. 'Oh no.'

Whetstone clutched at the fabric cutting into his neck, his face turning pink. 'It's not too late – you can still let us go. I'm pretty important, you see. Odin sent me on this quest—'

Lotta looked up. 'We don't have time for this. We need to get out of here.'

'Good luck,' Snotra snorted as Jormungandr's enormous coils rose from the choppy sea, encircling the longboat. The cat hissed as it skidded across the deck in its box.

Lotta narrowed her eyes. She thrust an elbow into the stomach of the crewman holding her. The man released her, gasping for breath. Lotta spun forward, grabbing Whetstone and yanking him away from his captor. With the sound of ripping fabric, Whetstone was freed. He stumbled forward, feeling pretty amazed by Lotta's impressive new moves.

Lotta's warhorse trotted forward, the damaged deck bouncing under his hooves. 'Thighbiter, wait!' Lotta yelped, tripping over her own feet as she grabbed at his bridle. Whetstone helped her up – he should've known her slick moves were too good to last. The horse's neck stretched out, reaching for something.

Whetstone gazed into the air above the horse's head. Something glittered there. 'Is that an . . . apple?'

'Don't be ridiculous; fruit doesn't fly,' Bragi began with a sniff.

'A toenail boat is fine, but a flying apple – *that's* too much?' Whetstone retorted.

With a shimmer, a silver-haired girl on horseback appeared hovering in mid-air, an apple in her outstretched hand. A smug smile on her face.

Bragi's mouth dropped open. The other Vikings gawped.

'Flee!' Lotta stared in shock.

The girl rose higher. Before Lotta could do anything to stop him, Thighbiter sprang into the air after the apple, sending Lotta crashing into Bragi. Then, with a *pop*, Flee and Thighbiter disappeared.

The Vikings gasped.

'Thighbiter, you come back here right now!' Lotta's knuckles cracked as her hands clenched into fists. 'Flee! You are going to be in so much trouble when I tell Scold what you've done!'

Whetstone blinked a few times. Things were happening too quickly for him to make sense of them. Blood pounded in his ears as the realization sank in that they'd lost their only means of escape.

Lotta spun round to face Snotra. 'You'd better tell us what is going on right now!'

The gold tooth glinted in Snotra's smile.

With a waft of cheesy feet, Naglfar drew up alongside them. Slightly transparent and ghostlike, it bobbed easily in the waves. Its sides and hull were woven out of thousands upon thousands of tiny slithers of nail. Whetstone stared, weirdly impressed that toenails made such good boat-building material. A tattered rope with a hook on the end landed at Whetstone's feet. Whetstone stared at it, disgusted. 'What's this made of? Eyebrows?'

A grey-skinned man jumped across from Naglfar, following the rope, tattered clothes hanging from his withered body. Whetstone ducked behind Lotta. The man hauled on the rope to drag the boats closer together.

'Naglfar is crewed by the dead.' Lotta smacked the man with her sword, knocking him into the water. 'Don't let them touch you or you'll end up like them!'

More hooks were flung on to the ship, swiftly followed by more dead sailors.

'Snotra has doomed all of you!' Lotta yelled at the longboat crew. 'You have to help us – push the sailors in the water and keep away from the toenail boat!'

Jormungandr tightened his coils; the boat squealed.

'Where's the cat?' Lotta panted, whacking another dead sailor with her sword.

'Forget the cat.' Whetstone dodged past the Viking crew, now busy battling dead sailors. 'We've got bigger problems!'

Rising easily through the sea spray on the tip of Jormungandr's tail, Loki appeared. Sunlight glinted off the golden threads in his tunic, making him look like a figure from a dream. If Whetstone hadn't seen him being swallowed by the dragon with his own eyes, he would've doubted anything bad had ever happened to him. His fine clothes and handsome looks were intact, apart from the scars that twisted his mouth – souvenirs of an old deal gone wrong with the Dwarves.

He landed easily on the deck, stepping through the chaos as though it were nothing. 'Hello, Whetstone.' Before Whetstone could open his mouth to speak, Lotta stepped forward. 'I should've known. You're getting Flee and Flay to do your dirty work again. What was it this time? Were they jealous that I won the contest?'

Loki smiled, his lips twisting. 'I might have *friends in high places*, but I haven't asked Flee or Flay to do anything for me. Someone else has plans for you, Lotta.'

Lotta glared.

Loki fixed his dark eyes on Whetstone. 'Come with me now or die. There is no other way off this boat.'

Snotra clambered across the deck towards them. 'Loki promised to take me to new worlds,' she puffed. 'Join us, kid. Adventure Awaits!'

The cat, still in its box, bumped into Whetstone's ankles, making him jump. 'OK, OK. I'll go.' Lotta's brown eyes opened wide. Whetstone spoke quickly. 'But first I have a present for you.' He scooped up the box and wrenched it open, allowing the enraged cat to spring out.

Huge, with brown-and-white fluff and a face like a furry fist, the cat attached itself to the man's head, spitting furiously. Loki cried out as all four sets of claws dug into his skin. Snotra tried to wrench it away and got a set of claws to her face for her trouble.

Lotta giggled. 'Nice one.'

Hearing Loki's cries of pain, Jormungandr squeezed his body tighter round the longboat. Whetstone slipped as the deck buckled beneath his feet.

'STOP!' Lotta yelled. 'Stop! I'm going to tell Odin—'

With a great boom, the sail came crashing down, covering the ship with canvas. Lotta dived out of the way, crashing through the fractured boat and into the cold ocean.

'LOTTA!' Whetstone threw himself at the side of the boat.

A head with thick black hair bobbed to the surface. Whetstone almost collapsed with relief. 'I'll get you out of there!'

He looked around what was left of the wooden longboat. Great cracks split the sides and most of the crew were missing. Whetstone tried not to think about what had happened to them. Loki and the cat were nowhere to be seen. He grabbed a coil of rope, quickly looping one end round the snarling figurehead before throwing the other end towards Lotta.

Lotta thrashed in the water, weighed down by her armour. Each time she dipped under the waves it took her longer to resurface.

'C'mon,' Whetstone muttered. 'Find the rope.'

Hands grabbed him from behind. Snotra snarled at Whetstone, her face covered in painful scratches. 'You can't stop us!'

Whetstone twisted away. 'There is no "*us*"! He'll leave you out here to die.'

The ship creaked, jagged peaks appearing as the floorboards splintered apart. The boy grabbed hold of the grimacing figurehead and swung himself out, dangling over the water, away from Snotra's grasping fingers.

Something tugged on his foot. Jormungandr had taken hold of his boot and was peeling him away from the boat. Whetstone kicked out wildly and his too-big boot slid off and vanished into the sea monster's mouth.

With a crunch, the boat finally gave up. Water rushed to fill enormous holes in the sides. Jormungandr roared, sinking into the dark water, dragging the rear of the boat down with him. Whetstone clung on as the figurehead was thrust high into the air, his fingers slipping on the greasy wood. The last few Vikings dived into the water to try to escape being taken down with the sinking ship.

The figurehead splintered, plunging Whetstone into the cold ocean. He gasped in shock and immediately swallowed a huge mouthful of seawater before a frothing wave dragged him down.

Whetstone wasn't a strong swimmer. In fact, he wasn't much of a swimmer at all. Having had a nasty experience growing up in Drott, when some of the older boys had thrown him into the lake, he usually tried to avoid the water completely.

Whetstone's head broke the surface, gasping for breath once more, his clothes and remaining boot weighing him down. He kicked off the boot and tried with numb fingers to undo his cloak. Bragi floated past, clinging to a piece of broken mast. Whetstone kicked out awkwardly towards him, but before he'd gone more than a couple of yards, a cold, clammy hand grabbed his arm.

Whetstone spun in the water – a wave smacked him in the face. When his vision cleared, he saw Lotta, soaking wet but safe, sitting on a raft of broken timbers. With difficulty, she hauled him up to join her as he floated past.

'Th-th-th-thanks, Lotta.'

Freyja's big fluffy cat was curled up on the raft with them, its fur dark with seawater. It licked a paw and screwed up its face at the taste.

'You saved the cat, then.' Whetstone grinned through blue lips.

The raft bumped into something. Whetstone looked up as *Naglfar* loomed over them, the toenail sides giving the boat a pearly sheen. Dead sailors gripped the oars, keeping the boat steady in the choppy water. With a crack of green light, Loki reappeared on the boat. The cat hissed, its hackles rising.

Loki leaned over the side of the ship, his face covered in scratches. He stretched out a hand. 'Come with me – I'll take you to dry land.'

Whetstone leaned away. 'No way. I'm not going anywhere with you.'

The raft rocked as Lotta rose on to her knees. Her hand fumbled behind her, but found only an empty scabbard. Her sword was gone.

'You only want to help because you think I know the riddle,' Whetstone began.

'I *know* you know the riddle,' the man replied, still smiling.

'No, you don't,' Whetstone replied hotly. 'You weren't there. That all happened after the dragon ate you!'

Loki's smile widened. 'So you do know it. I thought as much.'

Whetstone spluttered in frustration.

'Nice one,' Lotta muttered. 'That was exactly the wrong thing to say.'

Loki lifted a bundle from by his feet, a shimmering golden harp frame with a carved figurehead poked out of the sack.

Whetstone's mouth went dry.

It was the Skera Harp.

'I found the harp frame in Niflheim. Tell me where the strings are, and I will take you to your parents.'

Whetstone found himself unable to look away from Loki's face. It was so tempting. All he wanted was his parents back. He didn't care *that* much about the harp strings themselves. But then Loki would have all that power . . . Whetstone blinked, trying to break the spell Loki had over him.

Odin had instructed Whetstone to find the harp strings before Loki could use them to break down the walls between the Nine Worlds. If Loki fixed the harp, he would be able to send all the monsters out of Whetstone's nightmares and into Midgard. Enormous wolves, dragons, Giants, sea monsters . . .

'Loki!' Snotra clung to the lid of a chest. She reached out a hand to the smiling man. 'Help me!'

Loki ignored her, still intent on Whetstone. The harp shifted in his arms. 'You're no Hero, Whetstone, despite what Odin might have told you. He's just using you because he's too lazy to do anything himself. But I want to help you. Just tell me the riddle and you'll be back with your parents by tomorrow.'

'Loki, please!' Snotra bobbed beneath the waves for a second, her grip slipping on the smooth wood. 'This isn't what we agreed!'

The scars around Loki's mouth twisted his smile into something unpleasant.

The water beneath them bubbled and seethed.

'Jormungandr!' Lotta seized a piece of broken wood, trying to paddle away.

'You promised me adventures in new lands!' Snotra's fingers slipped again.

Loki turned his dark eyes on the struggling woman. 'Indeed I did. Your adventures begin with Aegir's kingdom.'

'Aegir,' Whetstone muttered, glancing at Lotta. 'The Sea King?'

Lotta nodded as she paddled the raft in circles. 'His kingdom is filled with drowned sailors.'

'Loki, please, pull me up!' Snotra gasped, reaching out.

Loki leaned away. 'Goodbye, whatever your name was. Say hello to Aegir for me.'

A whirlpool opened and, with a sucking *pop*, Snotra vanished beneath the waves.

'Jormungandr ate her!' Whetstone spluttered.

Loki nodded. 'And you're next. Unless you join me now.'

Lotta grabbed Whetstone's shoulder, peering into his face. 'Don't listen to him. There's more than one type of Hero, remember?'

Whetstone could only nod, his head numb with cold and shock. A roaring sound filled his ears.

Loki reached towards him. 'There is no time. Come with me!'

'I don't think so, Loki,' Lotta declared. 'And you're wrong – there *is* another way out.'

She pointed at the northern horizon. A horizon that seemed a lot closer now. The roaring grew louder and Whetstone realized it wasn't just inside his head.

Lotta grinned. 'See you in another of the Nine Worlds!'

Loki grew pale. He placed the harp back down by his feet. 'You cannot be serious. Trying to pass between the worlds on a raft is madness!'

Whetstone jerked. 'Passing where in a what?'

Lotta got up on to her knees again. Holding on to Whetstone's shoulder for support, she punched one hand into the air. 'VALHALLA FOREVER!'

Caught in a riptide, the raft spun away from Loki and his boat of dead men. Whetstone's stomach heaved.

'Trust me,' Lotta shouted over the thundering water. 'And hold on to the cat!'

The raft tipped. Whetstone grabbed the ball of angry fur as they were thrown over the edge of Midgard and out into the unknown.

Chapter Six

Alfheim is Nice
this Time of Year

Back in Asgard, Flay led Thighbiter into the stables. The horse whickered at the unfamiliar Valkyrie. 'Shhh. Look, you're home now – everything is back to normal.'

Thighbiter tossed his mane. Usually Lotta gave him apples after a long flight, but apart from the one this silver-haired girl had given him, there didn't seem to be any more coming. Thighbiter sneezed at her, showering the girl with bogeys. Flay gagged.

'The horse is as disgusting as Lotta,' Flay's sister Flee remarked, stuffing hay into Thighbiter's stall. 'Good thing she's gone.' On Thighbiter's back, Lotta's shield shimmered gently.

The stable door opened behind them. 'Come on, girls. Only villains lurk in the shadows.'

Flee smirked and followed the sound of the voice outside into the courtyard. Flay followed, raking her fingers through her bogey-filled hair.

Glinting-Fire ticked her clipboard with her pencil. 'The horse is back – good. We can't have valuable assets like that left behind.' She looked up at the two girls, her thick black plaits sticking out on either side of her helmet. 'And the, ahem, defect?'

'We followed her to Midgard.' Flee tossed her head. 'She landed on the boat, so we took the horse and left her there. Jormungandr has probably eaten her by now.'

Glinting-Fire scribbled something on her clipboard. 'I am still amazed that she fell for that ridiculous story about the cat being a gift for Njord.'

Flay gave up on her bogey-encrusted plait and tossed it over her shoulder. 'Is it true you stole Freyja's cat because she told everyone your porridge tasted like cat litter?'

Glinting-Fire's eyes narrowed. 'Two problems; one stone.'

Flay gulped.

Glinting-Fire held her gaze. 'Where is the cat now? Did you bring it back like you were supposed to?'

Flee and Flay looked at each other. 'Um—'

Glinting-Fire pursed her lips. 'Freyja is not going to be happy. It was only supposed to go missing for a short while, not permanently!'

Pink spots appeared on the twins' cheeks.

'I don't have time for these mistakes; we're on a very tight schedule.' Glinting-Fire tutted. She strode across the courtyard.

Flay scurried after her, her hand raised. 'Err, excuse me. Glinting-Fire?'

The short Valkyrie stopped. Flay almost crashed into her heels. 'What is it?'

'Why *exactly* did you want to get rid of Lotta? I mean, if it's not rude to . . . ask . . .' Flay trailed to a halt as Glinting-Fire glared, the tattooed lines on her face scrunching up.

'Change is coming. The Nine Worlds will be reordered and I intend for the Valkyries to take their rightful place at the top,' the tiny Valkyrie said carefully.

Flee looked at Flay in confusion. 'What does that mean? Odin is at the top.'

'I have an arrangement with someone,' Glinting-Fire continued, 'who understands that for things be rebuilt they must first be destroyed. The present system is . . . due an upgrade. This is our opportunity to show the Nine Worlds our true power.' Glinting-Fire took a step towards the twins. 'As ambitious young ladies, I'm sure you understand that there are still a few loose ends to tie up before we can go public with the plan. Your assistance will of course be rewarded.'

Flee and Flay glanced at each other and nodded.

'Wonderful. I can immediately see that you are obviously Class Two material.'

The twins preened.

Glinting-Fire smiled. 'Of course, not all Valkyries are as clever as you two: some will need to be shown the errors of their ways and brought to the true path. Others, like the unfortunate Lotta, will need to be removed entirely in order to let us all flourish.'

Flee wrinkled her nose. 'So you got rid of Lotta because she's a rubbish Valkyrie?'

'I have great ambitions for the Valkyries,' Glinting-Fire continued. 'Under my leadership we can make the Hero system much more efficient. But for us to advance there are some *consequences* for Midgard.'

'Oh,' said Flay, understanding. 'Lotta helped that smelly human boy. You thought she'd tip Midgard off about your plans!'

Glinting-Fire sniffed. 'Valkyries shouldn't fraternize with humans. We are far greater than them.'

'But we don't know for definite what happened to Lotta.' Flee bit her lip. 'Shouldn't we check?'

Glinting-Fire gave a tiny smile. 'Did you bring back the girl's shield?'

Flay nodded.

Glinting-Fire tucked her clipboard under her arm and marched back to the stables. Despite her small size, she moved very quickly and often in unexpected directions, like a ferret that had been stung by a wasp. Thighbiter curled his lip at the sight of them.

Flay strode to the horse and grabbed the circular shield. 'Ow!' She dropped it, sucking her burning fingers. 'It's red hot!' Thighbiter stamped his hoof.

Glinting-Fire poked the fallen shield with her pencil. 'A shield is connected to the Valkyrie who owns it. You can't be a Valkyrie without a shield. If you're displaying strong Valkyrie skills, your shield will glow brightly. If you're failing, they're dull.'

'And if they're red hot?'

Glinting-Fire prodded it again. 'Clearly Jormungandr didn't eat Lotta. We need to break the bond between this shield and the girl as soon as possible.'

'But then Lotta wouldn't be a Valkyrie any more,' Flee spluttered.

Flay trod on her sister's toe. 'That's kind of the point, dummy. If she likes humans so much, she might as well go and be one.'

'Flee? Flay?' boomed a voice from the courtyard. 'Where are you?'

The twins peered out to see the mighty Scold standing with her hands on her hips, gazing around. Her breastplate glinted in the sunlight. The twins turned pale.

Flay whispered, 'What about Scold? She will never understand. She'll try to stop you.'

'Scold has lost her edge,' Glinting-Fire muttered. 'I've been softening her up for weeks.' The short Valkyrie gave Flee and Flay a calculating look. 'Why don't we see if you two can finish the job?'

Flee gulped.

Glinting-Fire marched over to Scold and prodded her on the hip with her pencil. 'Good – you're here. I'm checking up on the stables. Do you always leave them in such a mess?'

Scold sucked in a breath. 'What mess?'

'To start with, the bridles aren't straight, there are cobwebs on the blankets and that horse needs to be mucked out.' She glanced over her shoulder at Flay. 'Get on with it, would you, girl?'

Flay kicked some hay over the fallen shield. Smoke curled up from where the hay touched it.

Scold pulled herself up to her full height. 'Glinting-Fire, you need to watch your tone. In case you have forgotten, you are not Leader of the Valkyries. *I* am.'

Glinting-Fire squinted up at the larger woman. 'And *I* am in charge of Discipline and Order in the Valkyrie ranks.'

Scold's nostrils flared.

'I can see why Odin wanted me to keep an eye on you.' Glinting-Fire scribbled something on her clipboard. 'Standards are slipping and that cannot continue.'

Scold's olive face turned pink. 'I have had no complaints—'

'More Discipline and Order. That's what this place needs.' Glinting-Fire tapped her pencil decisively on her clipboard. 'What other things have been getting on top of you recently? You'd better tell me so I can sort them out before things get any worse.'

Scold's jaw clenched.

Flay took a deep breath and ducked past Glinting-Fire to take Scold's arm. 'Scold, we all know that you're the Leader of the Valkyries and you're a brilliant teacher, but everyone needs a rest from time to time. When did you last have a holiday?'

'A holiday? Valkyries don't take holidays,' Scold spluttered.

'Well, maybe they should,' said Flee, forcing a look of sympathy on to her face and joining her sister. She dropped her voice. 'I wasn't going to say anything, but I did hear Odin talking after the poetry contest. He seemed worried you were letting things slip. It's only natural that things get missed when you work as hard as you do.'

Flay nodded, her voice low. 'So why not take this opportunity to have a little rest? Put your feet up. Let Glinting-Fire do some work for a change.'

'Put my feet up? What are you two on about?'

Flee moved closer. 'Glinting-Fire is always hanging around Valhalla with her clipboard. When was the last time she served mead?'

'Or recited some poetry?'

'Or brought back a fallen warrior?'

Scold's brow furrowed as she considered this. 'You might have a point.'

Flay nodded, her uneven plaits bouncing up and down. 'Exactly. Remind everyone of how hard you work –'

'– by not working for a bit,' Flee agreed. 'Everyone will soon come crawling back to you. There's no way Glinting-Fire will be able to do your job – she'd soon muck it up.'

The trio peered back at the tattooed Valkyrie. A pencil smudge ran up the side of her face. Flee sniggered.

'Oh, all right. I have been meaning to visit Alfheim. Maybe I will ask Odin for a few days off.' Scold prised her arms away from the twins. 'But I want to see Lotta as soon as she gets back from Midgard. How long can it take to deliver a parcel? Did Glinting-Fire give it to her all right?'

Flay nodded. 'Oh yes. And as soon as Lotta gets back we'll let you know.'

With a last *harrumph*, Scold left the twins. Flee squeezed Flay's hand. As Scold's shadow vanished through the archway, the girls skipped back to Glinting-Fire.

'We did it.'

'She's gone!'

Glinting-Fire looked at them appraisingly. 'I never realized quite how cunning you two were.' The twins smirked. 'We will need a more permanent solution for Scold eventually, but let's focus on the girl for now.'

'What do you want us to do?' Flee peered through the stable doorway at Lotta's shield. A black ring of charred hay was forming round it. 'Maybe if we leave it, it'll burst into flames or something?'

The tattooed Valkyrie marched into the stables and handed Flee a pair of dragonhide gloves from off the shelf. 'The connection is stretching. We need to break it. Someone else needs to claim ownership of the shield. Someone powerful.'

Flee twisted the gloves between her fingers. 'But even if we give the shield away, it won't be enough to stop Lotta being a Valkyrie.'

Glinting-Fire looked up sharply. 'I'm not talking about *giving* it away. Someone has to *take* it. We can't afford to be wishy-washy about these things. Powerful magic binds a Valkyrie shield to its owner. The only way to break it is by force.'

Flee bit her lip. 'But who is strong enough to take a shield away from a Valkyrie?'

'I'll leave that up to you.' Glinting-Fire tucked the pencil into her clipboard. 'The longer the shield is out of Lotta's possession, the weaker she will grow, until eventually the connection will break entirely.' Glinting-Fire smiled again. 'Take a Valkyrie shield away from its owner and you'll be surprised what you can do.'

'What do you mean?' Flee asked nervously.

'Aren't you curious about how I will ensure the other Valkyries fall in with my plan?' Glinting-Fire smirked. 'They won't have a choice. If I control all the shields, they can either join me, or stop being Valkyries.'

Flee gasped, her hands over her mouth.

Flay gulped. 'Scold's not gone forever,' she warned.

'Not yet.'

'And if Lotta gets her shield back before the connection breaks she'll still be a Valkyrie.'

'Then you'd better get a move on.' Glinting-Fire nudged a wide box half covered in straw with her toe. 'Get rid of Odin's real package for Njord while you're at it.' She turned on her heel. 'I'm going to go help Scold pack for her holiday. I'll open the gates for you, but you'll need to be back before nightfall. I can only cover for you until then.' The tiny Valkyrie marched out of the stables.

Flee pulled on the dragonhide gloves, scales glinting on her fingers. She passed a second pair to her sister. 'Come on. Let's get this thing out of here.' She gripped one side of

Lotta's shield and lifted it off the smoking hay.

Flay grabbed the other side. Between the two of them, they managed to get the shield out into the courtyard. 'Where shall we take it?'

'You heard what Glinting-Fire said – we have to find someone powerful.'

Chapter Seven

Over the Edge

'VAAALLLHALLLLLAAA FOREVEEEEEEER!'

The boy, girl and cat plunged over the side of Midgard in an enormous waterfall. Bits of broken ship and even a few fish fell with them. Whetstone clutched the cat to his chest with one hand, flailing in the air with the other. The cat screeched and clung on with all four sets of claws. Wind and water poured past Whetstone's face, choking him whenever he tried to breathe.

In the gaps between the terror, images flashed into Whetstone's mind: Snotra's face as she sank beneath the waves, Loki's hand reaching out for him, Jormungandr's mouth gaping open. Whetstone shook his head, amazed that he could have been so stupid as to trust Ulf or Snotra or whoever she was. Loki almost caught him. Whetstone resolved not to make that mistake again. From now on, he was on his own.

He forced his eyes open. Spread out below them were the branches and roots of Yggdrasil, the great world tree. Perched here and there were the different worlds. Some green, others grey. Red sparks flew from one, and deep in the roots endless mists poured from another. He wondered if this was one of

the weak points Ulf had mentioned, where it was possible to cross from one world and into another, and in which world they might end up.

The streams of water were thinning now, giving Whetstone enough space to catch his breath. They tumbled past a world that looked like a hollowed-out mountain range. Tiny figures vanished into cracks and caves, lanterns winking out of the darkness. Whetstone nearly smacked into a heavily engraved sign hanging from a branch: *Svartalfheim. Payment Up Front.*

Beside him, Lotta screamed 'Dwarrrrrrrves!' over the sound of the wind and water. Whetstone tried to nod.

A cloud of steam engulfed them. Whetstone spluttered and choked as the smell of rotten eggs hit the back of his throat. Red sparks flew up, burning his white skin where they landed. Whetstone rubbed his cheek, leaving behind a smear of charcoal. The cat clung on grimly, its fluffy fur sticking straight up.

'MUSPELL!' Lotta yelled as they dropped past a world of black grit and fiery volcanos. Down, down, down.

There were only two worlds left below them now. A pair of signs hung from nearby roots, each pointing down into the murk. One read *Niflheim: It's Too Late*, and the other *Helheim: Lost and Found*. On the most distant world, a red blob, hazy through thick mists, grew larger. The blob wiggled, unfurling bat-like wings. A spurt of flame followed.

'Nidhogg!' Whetstone yelped. The cat dug its claws deeper into his arm. Nidhogg was the dragon Whetstone had accidentally woken by dropping what was left of the Skera

Harp on him during their last adventure, and who had gone on to eat Loki. Nidhogg lived in Niflheim, the lowest of all the worlds.

Whetstone twisted towards the other world, making swimming motions in the air. This one had to be Helheim. If falling off Midgard meant he could make it to Helheim before Loki, this nightmare might just be worth it.

Lotta grabbed his foot. 'What are you dooooooooooooing?'

'HEEEELLL-HEIIIIIM!' Whetstone bellowed, ignoring the cat, whose claws must've been embedded in his bones by now.

Lotta let go of his foot, her face screwed up in concentration. Whetstone recognized that look. Valkyries could transform into birds. Last time, to save them both from the dragon, Lotta had turned into a sort of . . . duck-thing.

There was a loud *pop* and a shower of feathers, but Lotta hadn't transformed. The Valkyrie looked down at herself in confusion, then screwed up her face again. With a crack of blue light, Lotta changed, but she wasn't a bird. Instead, large wings had sprouted out of her back. They caught an updraft and Lotta shot upwards.

Whetstone tumbled on, trying to dodge the twisting roots. Helheim opened up in concentric circles below him like a huge eye. Green, blue, white and dusty brown. A Great Hall sat in the middle as the dark pupil. At least they were heading towards the right world. Whetstone just hoped they had something soft for them to land on.

In a streak of blue light and a flurry of feathers, Lotta

reappeared beside him, her wings folded into a dive. Gritting her teeth, she grabbed Whetstone by his free arm – the one not being used as a claw sharpener. Their descent slowed, Lotta's wings beating hard to support all their weight. Whetstone's shoulder burned as if his arm was going to be ripped out of its socket.

'Hold on!' Lotta shouted. But the cat wasn't listening. It wiggled and thrashed, clawing at Whetstone's face. The boy tried to clamp it against his chest, but the cat fought its way free and leaped out into space. Whetstone thought he saw a smug expression on its furry face before it dropped out of sight.

'Nooo!' Lotta's grip slipped as she snatched at the cat. Whetstone tried to grab Lotta with his other hand, but his fingers found nothing but air. Then he was falling, heading straight for the bullseye of Helheim, Lotta hanging suspended above him.

✴

Water clanged in his ears. Whetstone's chest burned as he fought to hold his breath. He had dropped straight into an icy river! Currents tossed him head over heels until he no longer knew which way was up. His head pounded and every direction looked the same. Whetstone's chest throbbed. He needed air! With a massive effort, he hauled himself through the water until his head finally broke the surface.

He gasped down a huge lungful of air, but before he could get his bearings the river dragged him away. Whetstone flailed, trying to keep his head above water. A jagged outcrop of rocks loomed ahead of him.

On wobbly legs, Lotta landed on the riverbank, wings still sticking out of her back. 'Whetstone!'

He struck out towards her, fighting the pull of the river. Something bashed into his side. He gasped, choking a little as spray filled his mouth.

'Over here!' Lotta hung over the edge of the riverbank. She stretched out a broken tree branch for him to grab on to. Whetstone reached out, his fingers scraping the bark. Lotta gritted her teeth and dragged him through the icy water.

Whetstone pulled himself up the riverbank. Dripping wet, frozen, and very, very relieved to be alive. He collapsed next to Lotta, rolling on to his back, rubbing his hands over his face, his skin stinging with cold.

'I am never getting wet again,' the boy spluttered, air burning in his chest. 'Ever.'

Lotta massaged her shoulder. 'Where's the cat?'

'Dunno. Can Freyja's cats fly?' He turned his head to look at the Valkyrie; the wings on her back shimmered. 'Did you know that . . . wing thing . . . was going to happen? I know Odin said you might be a different type of Valkyrie, but it's a bit . . . odd.'

Lotta twisted round to peer at her wings. 'It's never happened before. I was trying to turn into a bird.'

'It's good, though.' Whetstone nodded. 'Must be handy having arms as well as wings.'

With a loud *pop*, the wings vanished. Lotta untied her hair and started trying to squeeze the water out. 'Why is it that whenever I'm with you I end up plummeting to my doom?'

Whetstone picked a clump of damp cat hair off his tunic. 'Your good luck, maybe?'

Lotta snorted.

A warm breeze drifted past, drying his wet clothes. Whetstone felt the urge to close his eyes. 'You know, this isn't what I imagined the Land of Lost Things to be like,' he said with a yawn. 'I thought it would be all icy and dark.'

'It is,' Lotta replied, retying her hair into its usual puff. 'Over there.' She gestured to the other side of the riverbank.

Whetstone lifted his head. The side of the river they had landed on was warm and green with plants. On the opposite side, black and stumpy trees sprouted out of thick snow, their branches empty and bleak. A red sun hung low in the sky. The boy shivered and dropped his head back into the grass.

'That's where Hel lives. And it's where your dad and the harp string are.'

Whetstone swallowed. '*One you will find below, in an ice-locked land, Still living but alone, for Hel holds him in her hand,*' he recited.

'It certainly looks ice-locked to me,' Lotta said with a bit of a grin. She gave him a playful shove. 'Just think, your dad is over there. You could be about to meet him!'

Whetstone closed his eyes, a heavy lump settling in his chest: a ball of excitement, fear and anxiety. His mind tingled at the thought of rescuing his father and finding the first harp string.

He bit his lip, hoping that Loki hadn't got there ahead of them. Loki had spent twelve years fruitlessly searching for the harp strings, waiting for Whetstone to get the riddle and reveal the clues. If Loki had been unable to find the harp strings so far, they must be well hidden.

Whetstone pushed himself to his feet. 'Come on – let's go.'

A rattling noise came from something in the distance.

'Wait, what's that?'

Chapter Eight

Lost and Found

Several worlds above Whetstone and Lotta, a pair of massive warhorses pounded through the air. They carefully followed the huge trunk of Yggdrasil, the world tree, dropping lower and lower. Eventually, they soared over the mines of the Dwarves and around the volcanos of Muspell.

Flee stopped next to a pair of twisted signs, her horse beating time with his hooves. Only two worlds lay beneath them. 'Niflheim or Helheim?'

Flay caught up with her sister. She glanced at the shield strapped to her saddle. Even though they had wrapped it in old sacks, Flay could still feel the heat rising off it. 'I don't care as long as I can get rid of this thing. It shouldn't be hot like this.'

Flee sniffed. 'Stop complaining. You're carrying the shield; I'm carrying Njord's package. Fair's fair.' Flee peered down into the roots. 'Niflheim is the furthest from Asgard.'

Flay rubbed her nose, which was going pink from the chill. 'Glinting-Fire said to give it to someone powerful. Who is powerful in Niflheim?'

'Let's find out.' Flee shook her reins, her horse plunging towards the world far below.

Flay sighed. She pushed her helmet down over her uneven plaits and urged her horse down, following her sister.

A land of fog and shadow, Niflheim was the lowest and darkest of all the Nine Worlds. It was one of the two worlds in which Vikings (who had not been chosen to enter Valhalla) could find themselves after death. Helheim took those who had died peacefully, but Niflheim was the ultimate destination of those who had died in embarrassing or cowardly ways. Now these unfortunate Vikings roamed the endless mists, telling each other lies about their lives on Midgard and trying to avoid Nidhogg the dragon, who liked to chew on them.

Flee's horse landed lightly on the scrubby ground. The air was colder here. She shivered into her armour. 'Lose the shield and let's go. This place gives me the creeps.'

Flay squinted around. 'We have to *give* it to someone. It's the only way to break the bond.'

'But there's no one here,' Flee whined. 'Let's just leave it. Lotta will never find it in Niflheim.'

A hand with grey skin gripped Flay's leg. 'Preeetty lady,' a voice wheedled. Flay lurched back in shock. 'Give it to me, whatever it is. I was powerful once.'

'You liar,' called a second voice from out of the murk. 'The only thing powerful about you is the smell. I'll take it, lady. I was a king when I was alive.'

The grey hand let go of Flay's leg. 'No, you weren't. You lived in the next village to me. You were a turnip farmer.'

91

'They were better turnips than you ever grew!'

'Oh yeah?'

'Yeah!'

Flay edged her horse away from the bickering voices. She looked around. 'Flee?' Her sister had vanished. Forms moved in the mist. More and more of the grey figures appeared, smoke and shadows distorting their shapes. They shuffled towards Flay, forming a ragged circle round her. Flay's horse pawed at the ground. She twisted around in her saddle, trying to see all the ghostly figures at once. 'Flee! Where are you!'

A bow-legged man with an impressive moustache limped towards her. 'Ah, young lady. I insist that you give me your horse,' he said pompously. 'There was a mistake, you see. I shouldn't be here. I was supposed to go to Valhalla.'

Flay gripped on to her reins as the man tried to pull them away. 'Get lost. You're not a Hero.'

The man snarled, 'Don't you know who I am?'

'Flee!' Flay wailed, trying to back away.

Flee's horse reared through the shadows. 'No, I do not want to join your team by selling herbal skin-care lotions to my friends and family!' the girl screeched to someone behind her. Flee's horse crashed into the pompous man with the moustache, sending him flying. 'I think the shield is attracting them,' she panted.

'I can smell magic,' an elderly voice cackled.

'I don't care what Glinting-Fire said – I'm not giving Lotta's shield to any of this lot,' Flay huffed. 'There's no one powerful here, anyway.'

In the distance came a roar.

A ball of fire shot into the air. The sisters looked at each other with wide eyes.

'You upset Nidhogg!' Flee shrieked. Her horse leaped into the air.

Moments later, Flay rose out of the mists beside her. Below them, the ghostly Vikings scattered, vanishing into the gloom to hide from the dragon.

'Should we give the shield to Nidhogg?' Flee panted. 'He's powerful.'

The twins turned to face the flashes of fire in the distance.

'You do it. I'm not going near that thing,' Flay spluttered.

Nidhogg roared again, illuminating the swirling roots of Yggdrasil with a jet of fire.

'Let's go to Helheim.' Flee shuddered. 'I wouldn't stay here for all the dead warriors in Midgard!'

They headed back into the roots of Yggdrasil and on to Helheim, racing over the multicoloured landscape: green, blue, white and brown. Flay reined in her horse, hovering over the Great Hall in the centre of the world.

'Let's just drop the shield.' She pouted. 'I'm not going anywhere near the ground again.'

Flee wrinkled her nose. 'But Glinting-Fire said—'

'I don't care what Glinting-Fire said! If she wants to come all the way down here and *hand* the shield to someone, she can do it herself. Why don't we put a bow on it while we're at it?'

Flee hesitated for a moment before leaning over to her sister's saddle and cutting the ropes holding the shield with a short knife. The shield, still wrapped in sackcloth, slipped away from the horse and tumbled to the land below.

'Let's dump Njord's package on the way back. If anyone asks why it's in Helheim, we can say it *got lost*.'

❋

Several hours later, just as night fell, the twin Valkyries landed, exhausted, in front of the great gates of Asgard. A small shadow detached itself from the inside of the gates. It produced a clipboard. 'Is it done?'

Flay nodded, too tired to speak.

Beside her, Flee said through a yawn, 'They're in Helheim.'

Glinting-Fire nodded, opening the gates with an iron key. 'That should do it. Hel's power mad. She'll never give the shield back to Lotta.'

The girls and horses wearily slipped inside.

They were not unnoticed, however. A beautiful woman with a necklace that glowed in the gloom straightened up. 'What are you three doing out here?'

'We could ask you the same question, Freyja,' Glinting-Fire sniffed. 'Haven't you got some perfect porridge to make?'

Freyja put her hands on her hips. 'I'm looking for my cat – he never normally stays out this late. I've used magic to track him this far, but then the trail vanishes.'

'It must've snuck out through the gates,' Glinting-Fire said brusquely. 'You should take better care of your pets.'

'Here, kitty, kitty, kitty! Time for din dins!' Freyja called.

A crackle of red light shot out of the Goddess's hands, tracing a path along the ground. 'See, it goes out through the gates, then nothing.'

A shape appeared in the murk just outside the gates.

'Wait, there *is* something out there,' Flee murmured.

'Lost your cat, Freyja?' Loki asked, stepping through the archway and brushing back his golden hair. 'I do hope nothing has happened to it.'

Freyja curled her lip.

'Loki!' Flay laughed, suddenly energized. 'Where have you been?'

'And why are you all wet?' Flee added.

A cloud of green light and steam filled the air, making everyone cough. Loki emerged, now dry, from the cloud.

'Yuck, Loki fumes.' Freyja grimaced. Holding her sleeve over her nose, the Goddess backed away. Red light flashed and crackled as she continued calling for her cat.

Glinting-Fire stepped forward, her clipboard tucked under her arm. 'Loki, I've been waiting for you. Ready for Phase Two?'

A smile appeared on the handsome man's face.

Chapter Nine

Big Trouble

The rattling noises led Whetstone and Lotta away from the riverbank and into an open meadow. Well, it would have been open once. Now it was crammed full of apparently random things: weapons, jewellery, blankets, carved toys and musical instruments all jostled for space, forming heaps that towered over their heads.

Whetstone stopped in his tracks, amazed. 'What is all this stuff?'

Lotta shrugged. 'Helheim is the Land of Lost Things. These are the Lost Things.' Lotta ran her hand over an embroidered tunic. 'We need to find a way of getting in touch with Asgard. Someone is bound to have lost something we can use. Just look out for anything magical.'

Whetstone hesitated. A pocketful of golden coins rained down, landing with a ringing clatter inside a nearby metal helmet. Whetstone gazed at them longingly. Even though he had given up being a thief, gold still made his fingers itch. Lotta grabbed his arm.

'I was only looking!'

'Shhh!' The girl crept forward, her eyes fixed on something in a pile of blankets.

'What is it?'

Lotta ignored him. Instead, she dived head first into the heap. Loud spitting, yowling and a sneeze followed. Lotta rolled out of the pile, clutching Freyja's cat to her chest. She got to her knees, looking happier than she had since they'd arrived. 'Got you.'

Whetstone laughed. 'I suppose we did lose it.'

The cat leaped out of Lotta's arms, landing halfway up a hill of odd socks and broken hairbrushes.

'Oi, come back!' Lotta scrambled after it, sending an avalanche of chess pieces sliding down the lower slopes.

'Do we really need the cat?' Whetstone called as she disappeared.

'Yes!' Lotta's voice bounced back to him, the sound distorting through a large bronze battle horn. 'Odin will be angry if I don't deliver it!'

Whetstone rolled his eyes – she had a point. He shuffled after her.

A heap of boat hooks and lost oars shifted, revealing a large silver coin perched in a nest of ropes. Whetstone picked it up, the metal cool and smooth in his fingers. Maybe this was the sort of thing Lotta was looking for; it looked kind of magical. He turned it over.

Find Whetstone.
He has the riddle.
Don't let him get away.
L

Whetstone dropped the coin as if it had turned red hot, his pulse thudding loudly in his ears. Suddenly he didn't want to be alone among the mountains of junk. 'Lotta, where are you?' He clambered up the heap of odd socks and slid down a mound of jingling spoons on the other side.

With a wave of relief, he spotted Lotta kneeling in a patch of grass. Whetstone hurried towards her. 'We need to get out of here. I just found—
What is *that*?'

Lotta was peering carefully into a wide, shallow bowl. It glowed with a warm light, casting strange shadows on to the girl's face.

Whetstone leaned over Lotta's shoulder to get a better look. The bowl was filled with a curious amber liquid, and, instead of his own grubby face reflected in it, a picture of a room appeared. Suddenly, the room vanished and a group of tents in a field replaced it. The cat purred and rubbed itself against the bowl; the liquid inside burbled.

The boy dropped to his knees. 'What is this thing?'

'It was in that box.' Lotta pointed at a broken wooden case. 'I landed on it when I was chasing the cat.'

Whetstone flipped the box over. The runes: *To Njord, from Odin* were carved into the lid.

Lotta rubbed her eyes. 'I think it's a scrying bowl. I've seen Frigg use one for fortune-telling.'

Whetstone sat back on his heels. 'We don't need to tell our fortunes! I know Loki is looking for me. I just found a coin with a message on it.' He swallowed. 'Do you think he's trying to reach Hel?'

'That would make sense,' Lotta muttered, still peering into the bowl. 'Where is the coin now?'

Whetstone glanced over his shoulder. 'I dropped it. I think we should focus on getting my dad and the harp string and getting out of here. Not messing around with weird bowls.' Whetstone tapped the rim of the bowl, sloshing the liquid.

Lotta poked him in the forehead. 'Think for moment, will you? It's obvious that something strange is going on. We were both lured to the exact same place in the ocean at the exact same time, where – miraculously – Loki turns up and horrible Flee steals my horse? That's not a coincidence.'

Whetstone shrugged. 'Snotra made a deal with Loki.'

'But who sent Flee? Someone in Asgard must be working with Loki, even after Odin told everyone to leave him alone.' Lotta tapped the bowl. 'If I can figure out how this works, we can use it to reach Scold. Don't you want to find out what is going on before we go marching into Helheim?'

Whetstone drummed his fingers on his knees. Most of the trouble they'd got into last time was from making decisions without having all the facts. 'All right, what do we have to do? I thought you had to eat weird herbs or go into a trance or something to do magic.'

Lotta snorted. 'You do that – I'll keep trying this.'

Whetstone looked around for inspiration, his thoughts spinning. 'Freyja is magic, right?'

'Yeah?'

'So maybe her cat is too?' Whetstone grabbed some loose fur off the cat's back and tossed it into the bowl. Immediately, the liquid started to fizz. A flash of red light nearly blew off their eyebrows, but then a bronze sky appeared in the liquid.

'I cannot believe that worked,' Lotta breathed, leaning closer.

A pair of dark caves appeared.

'I didn't know there were caves in Asgard,' muttered Whetstone.

Lotta shook her head. 'There aren't.' She reached out to touch the amber liquid. The image flickered, and the caves – twitched?

101

'Are those . . . nostrils?' Whetstone wrinkled up his own nose. 'Eurgh! Are we looking up someone's nose?'

The caves twitched again. The owner of the nose was turning her head. Long black hair twisted with gold thread blocked their view before being brushed aside by fingers covered in golden jewellery. The bottom of a graceful jaw and an ear appeared. A woman's laugh echoed up through the pool. The cat rubbed itself against the bowl and purred.

Lotta grabbed Whetstone's arm. 'It's Freyja!'

Whetstone lunged forward. 'Really? She's supposed to be the most beautiful woman who ever lived!'

Freyja's voice rippled out of the bowl. 'Go away, Loki. I'm busy.'

Whetstone flinched again.

Freyja continued speaking. 'If I'd found it, I wouldn't still be looking, *would I*?' A man's voice murmured in the background. Freyja's nostrils flared. 'No, you won't. I *know* you, Loki. Where have you been anyway?'

Lotta looked at Whetstone and mouthed, '*Inside a dragon's bum.*' Whetstone couldn't help but giggle. Lotta elbowed him in the ribs.

'Did you just laugh at me?' Freyja sounded irritated now. The bronze sky wobbled as she took a step forward. A sliver of Loki's face appeared in the pool as Freyja waggled a bejewelled finger at him. Whetstone and Lotta both shrank back. 'I know you're up to something with the Valkyries. Just stay out of my way.' Freyja spun on her heel and marched off.

'What does she mean, Loki is up to something with the

Valkyries?' Lotta hissed.

Whetstone shrugged.

The pool went dark as a hand loomed. The picture wobbled, and an upside-down woman's face appeared. Whetstone tried not to stare.

'Who's there?' she asked.

Lotta swallowed. 'Er, hi, Freyja.'

The woman scowled. 'YOU!' Lotta sat up straight and saluted. Whetstone tried to smile, but his lips got stuck to his teeth. 'How did you get into my necklace? Oh, never mind. Let me get inside.'

The pool returned to the picture of the dark caves. The bronze sky above them wobbled as the woman walked.

'What does she mean, inside her necklace?' Whetstone whispered to Lotta.

'Don't you know anything? Her necklace is magical. It was made for her by the Dwarves. We must be looking out of it.'

The picture dimmed as the woman stepped through a doorway. The sky was replaced by a high-arched ceiling. The bowl juddered as she removed the necklace.

Whetstone ran his sleeve over his face and tried to stick his hair down. Lotta looked at him and rolled her eyes.

Freyja's face reappeared, the right way up this time. '*Explain.*'

'Er, we found a scrying bowl,' Lotta began.

'Why is she wearing a dressing gown?' Whetstone whispered.

'I can hear you.' Freyja knotted the robe around her. 'I haven't been to bed yet. I was out all night looking for my cat.'

Lotta twisted her fingers together. 'Your cat? Well, it didn't quite make it to Njord, I'm afraid—'

Freyja's jaw visibly clenched. 'That cat is stolen property. You had better bring it back to me right now.'

Lotta's face scrunched up. 'Stolen? But Glinting-Fire said you gave it to her—'

'*I do not give away cats!*'

Lotta waved her hands. 'It's fine! The cat's fine, though!' She scooped up the purring animal. 'See? Achoo!' The cat wiggled out of her hands.

'Just don't tell her about you dropping it,' Whetstone muttered.

Freyja tossed her head. 'And you left that infuriating cup here. It keeps trying to give me biscuit recipes.'

Lotta bit her lip. 'Oh, er, so everyone knows about that?'

Whetstone wrinkled his nose. 'What cup?'

'I *borrowed* Awfulrick's cup to help me win the poetry contest.' Lotta avoided his eyes. 'Because I wanted to come back to Midgard to see you.'

'Oh.' The memory of Awfulrick mentioning that Lotta had left a message surfaced in Whetstone's mind. He'd forgotten how hard Lotta had worked to come back to Midgard.

'I was supposed to bring it back to Awfulrick,' Lotta gabbled, 'but it was enjoying itself in Asgard and—'

Freyja fixed her eyes on Lotta, golden threads sparkling in her hair. Lotta sputtered to a halt.

'You're in big trouble, young lady.'

Lotta hung her head. She was always in trouble. What else was new?

Freyja tutted. 'Stop looking like someone's just trod on your birthday cake. You're not in trouble with me.'

Lotta looked up. 'Is it Scold? It wasn't cheating, not really—'

'Scold isn't here – that's part of the problem!'

Lotta's eyebrows shot upwards. Scold was as much part of Asgard as Valhalla was. She was always there.

'Pay attention, both of you,' Freyja snapped. Whetstone sat up straight, trying to look attentive and efficient. 'Lotta, you were tricked. We've *all* been tricked. The poetry contest was fixed.'

Lotta's mouth fell open.

'Njord was waiting by the coast for his parcel – Glinting-Fire sent you to the wrong place on purpose,' Freyja continued. 'It was an excuse to get you out of Asgard.'

'Me? But why?' Lotta stammered.

Freyja sighed, making the liquid ripple. 'Because of him.'

Whetstone's cheeks grew hot.

'It shouldn't be me telling you this, but . . .' Freyja glanced over her shoulder. 'Something is going on with the Valkyries.' She held up a hand to prevent Lotta interrupting. 'I don't know *exactly* what, but Asgard is full of rumours. The short one with the tattoos and the clipboard is up to something. She's convinced Scold to go to Alfheim for a *holiday*.'

Lotta snorted with laughter. 'Scold – on *holiday*?' She had a sudden vision of the mighty Valkyrie sitting on a sun lounger, rubbing suntan lotion into her muscular arms.

Freyja snapped. 'With Scold gone, who is in charge of the Valkyries?'

'Odin, the Allfather, the Spear Shaker, the Terrifying One-Eyed—'

Freyja rolled her eyes. 'Yes, but who actually gives the orders? Who organizes everything?'

Lotta screwed up her face. 'Scold. And if she's gone . . . I guess Glinting-Fire would take over.'

Freyja nodded. 'Precisely. And now she's got Loki helping her.'

Lotta's brown eyes opened wide.

'But if this Glinting-Fire person is up to something with Loki, why hasn't Odin stopped her?' Whetstone asked.

'Odin has left Asgard.'

'WHAT?' Again?' Lotta cried.

'Oh, I've heard of this.' Whetstone leaned forward. 'Doesn't he go off for a wander around the Nine Worlds every so often?'

'That man is infuriating.' Freyja crossed her arms. 'You would think he'd take his responsibilities a bit more seriously. Loki fed him some ridiculous story about the Giants having magic mead, so he's gone off to Jotunheim to check. Normally Scold would send the Valkyries to keep an eye on him, but Glinting-Fire won't let anyone go. She's even got Valkyries guarding the gates so no one can leave Asgard without her say-so. She says Odin will come back when he's ready. Frigg has been going bonkers.'

'So, no Odin, no Scold, and Glinting-Fire is plotting with Loki to get rid of me?' Lotta quavered.

Whetstone scrunched up his face. 'But why? Lotta's not important.'

Lotta's nostrils flared.

Freyja waggled a finger. 'She is unique. How often do Valkyries make friends with humans?'

Whetstone sat up straight. 'So it's because of me – because I'm a Hero?'

Freyja ignored him. She fixed her eyes on Lotta. 'My guess is that Glinting-Fire is planning something to do with Midgard. She doesn't want you chatting with your BFF and spilling the beans.'

Lotta wrinkled her nose. 'I wouldn't say we were *best* friends—'

Freyja spoke over her. 'That's not all. She got rid of your shield too.'

Lotta gasped, her face taking on a greenish tinge. 'My shield?'

Freyja nodded. 'I overheard her talking to those snobby twins while I was looking for Mr Tiddles.'

The cat looked up at the sound of his name. Whetstone bit the inside of his mouth to keep himself from laughing. *Mr Tiddles!* Then he saw the expression on Lotta's face. 'What's the big deal?' He shrugged. 'It's only a shield. You can probably find a better one here along with a new helmet and sword.'

'*Only a shield?*' Lotta croaked. 'It's where my Valkyrie powers are stored. Without it, I'll stop being a Valkyrie and turn into . . . into . . .'

'Come on – you can say it,' Whetstone prompted.

'A living human!' Lotta snapped. 'That's why I couldn't transform into a bird properly and just got the wings. I'm not a real Valkyrie without my shield.'

'It could've been worse – you could've ended up with bird feet, or a tail!' Whetstone snickered. 'Come on – it can't be that bad.'

'Not that bad!'

Freyja sniffed. 'The silver girls said they gave it to Hel. You need to go to Helheim and fetch it, quickly. If not, you'll lose your powers and change permanently.'

'But we're in—' Lotta began.

'But you haven't said what Loki—' Whetstone started at the same time.

'What? I can't hear you.' The picture rippled, distorting Freyja's face. 'The connection is breaking. Get out of my necklace, get the shield and get home before it's too late. And don't forget to bring my cat!'

The amber liquid undulated and Freyja vanished.

Lotta tapped the surface of the liquid, sending out new ripples. 'Hello? HELLO?'

Only their bewildered faces stared back.

Whetstone sat back on his heels. 'I think she's gone.'

Lotta stood up, scooping the reluctant cat back into her arms. 'Achoo!' She wiped her nose on her wrist guard. 'What are we hanging around here for? Let's get over that river and get my shield.'

Whetstone stood up, brushing grass off his knees. 'Your shield, the harp string, my dad. At this rate, we're going to have to write a list.'

Lotta gave a grim smile. 'Then when I get back to Asgard I'm going to cut off Flay's other plait.'

Chapter Ten

Crossing the Bridge

Leaving the mountains of Lost Things behind, they returned to the rushing river. Whetstone reluctantly lugging the large, fluffy cat in his arms. He nearly tripped over Lotta as she stopped suddenly at the top of the riverbank. The water below them was filled with broken weapons. Rusted armour poked up here and there. A shield swirled past, caught in an eddy.

The cat shifted in Whetstone's arms. 'My foster mother once told me that to reach Hel you had to cross a river filled with weapons.'

'Yeah. And there's supposed to be a bridge, and a bridge keeper.' Lotta shuffled closer to the water, reaching for a long sword sticking out of the mud. 'We'll have to be stealthy so he doesn't tell Hel we're here.'

'Why? I know she's the Queen of the Dead, but she might be nice.'

Lotta squinted at him, a warm breeze lifting her black curls. 'You don't know who Hel is, do you?'

The boy shrugged.

'She's Loki's daughter.'

Whetstone froze. All the air vanished from his lungs. The cat dropped out of his arms, landing lightly on the ground. The boy leaned forward, put his hands on his knees and groaned.

'Hel is Loki's daughter, and the sea monster who tried to crush us is her brother,' Lotta continued, tugging at the stuck sword.

Whetstone rubbed his hands over his face. 'I feel sick.'

Lotta sniffed. 'We don't need to go near her. We'll sneak in, get your dad, find the missing harp string, get my –' she clenched her jaw – 'shield, then get out again.' With a final tug, the sword came free. Lotta squidged back up the riverbank. 'How can you not know this? Odin banished Hel to the Land of Lost Things, Jormungandr was cast into the seas around Midgard and Fenrir—'

'Who's Fenrir?' Whetstone looked up in horror. 'Don't tell me there are more of them.'

'Fenrir's the youngest. He's a gigantic wolf. There are three of them.'

'Four. Don't forget about Vali.' Whetstone straightened up. 'He left Krud just before I did.'

Lotta smirked. 'I told you he wasn't really stone. Loki turned him into a Troll.'

'Yeah, but *where* is he and why did he leave Krud? I thought he was running away because Loki was coming back, but now I'm not so sure.' Whetstone whipped his head round to peer over his shoulder. 'You don't think Loki sent him to follow us, do you?'

'What's wrong? Don't you fancy joining the Loki family reunion?' Lotta grinned.

'How can I put this? I'd rather eat my own teeth.'

The cat meowed and rubbed against Whetstone's leg. Whetstone scooped it up and took a deep breath. 'All right. Let's find this bridge and get it over with.'

❈

'Wow – that's what I call a bridge.'

The bridge stretched elegantly across the river in an unbroken arc. To Whetstone's eye, it seemed impossibly long and narrow. Thin walls enclosed a solid gold path, which glinted enticingly. A small hut, also gold, sat on the other side, sticking out of the snow like a dropped earring.

Whetstone sighed. He might have given up being a thief, but that much gold would be enough to tempt anyone back to a life of crime. It seemed so unfair that successful thieves were rewarded with pockets full of gold, while successful Heroes just got more and more quests. He buried his fingers in the cat's fur, wondering if he should've stayed a thief.

'I guess this is where we cross.'

'It's either that or swim.'

Lotta's boot met the bridge

and a loud *DO-I-I-ING* reverberated across the landscape. A man with a long beard and a faded cloak emerged from the hut on the other side of the river.

'Is that him?' Whetstone muttered, trying to keep hold of the wiggling cat. 'I thought a monster guarded Helheim. I was expecting someone . . . scarier.'

'Remember the plan,' Lotta whispered out of the corner of her mouth. 'You're dead. I'm dead. It was tragic.'

Whetstone dropped the cat and stuck his arms straight out in front of him, his hands dangling down at the wrists. He rolled his eyes back into his head and let his tongue hang out of his mouth.

'What are you doing?' Lotta hissed.

'Being dead.' Whetstone staggered forward.

'Is he OK?' the man called.

'Yeah,' Lotta called back. 'This much gold just has that effect on him.' She kicked Whetstone on the ankle, and he dropped his arms.

Together they shuffled across the golden bridge, following the cat. When they reached the centre of the river, the bridge gave a shudder. Whetstone's stomach lurched. A cold wind reached out for them, pulling at the end of Whetstone's hair and giving him goosebumps.

The guard watched them approach.

As they got closer, Whetstone realized the man had two round pieces of glass held by twisted metal in front of this eyes, making his eyes look flat and lifeless.

Whetstone nudged Lotta. 'What are those glass things?'

She lifted one shoulder in a shrug.

At the end of the bridge, Whetstone stepped reluctantly into the snow. His toes immediately froze. He wrapped his arms round himself and tried to stop his teeth from chattering.

The man peered at them through his glass lenses. 'You two took your time.' His beard twitched into a smile. 'Hey, this place is so popular people are usually dying to get in!'

Lotta groaned. 'Was that a joke? It was dreadful.'

The man's beard twitched again. 'I've got more. Hey, why do you never see a cow playing hide-and-seek? Because they're really good at it!'

Lotta tutted. Whetstone jiggled up and down to keep warm.

'Just the cat, is it? Very Egyptian.' The man eyed up Mr Tiddles. 'Did you bring nothing else with you?'

Whetstone's face scrunched up in confusion. 'Like what?'

'Horses, treasures, fine cloth?' the man suggested. 'Whatever you were buried with, really. Traditionally, you're supposed to bring me a Hel-cake.'

Lotta glanced at Whetstone. 'Um . . . ?'

The man squinted at them. 'You're a bit young, aren't you? What was it that finished you off?'

'I was trampled by a crazed horde of – hedgehogs,'

Whetstone invented, his teeth chattering. 'They prickled me to death.'

'And I was picked up by a really *big* bat, who dropped me on some rocks,' Lotta lied. 'It was sooo painful when I landed.'

The man nodded sagely. 'You have to be careful of wildlife. Not that we get much of that here. I did see a couple of flying horses not long ago, though. Hey, what do you call a horse that lives next door? Your neigghhh-bour!'

Lotta spun towards him. 'Flying horses?' she gasped, grabbing hold of the man's tunic. 'Did they land anywhere? Were there two girls with armour like mine?'

The man stumbled back in surprise. 'They didn't land anywhere. Just dropped a big round thing and a box, then flew off again.'

'My shield!' Lotta wheezed. 'Where did they drop it?'

The man prised Lotta off his tunic. 'I'm not sure. The round thing landed somewhere in the snowfields between here and the Great Hall. I couldn't see where the box went.'

'Brilliant! Maybe my shield's still in the snow. We won't have to go anywhere near Hel!'

'Why don't you want to see Hel?' the man asked, surprised. 'Most people want to at least meet her.'

Lotta glared. 'I'm just . . . really shy.'

'Well, to get it back, you'll have to talk to her.' The man's beard twitched into a frown. 'I'm afraid the Helhest took it.'

Lotta's forehead crinkled. 'Who are the Helhest?'

'And why does Hel keep naming everything after herself?'

115

Whetstone muttered, jiggling from foot to foot. 'It's very confusing.'

The man looked at him sideways. 'The Helhest is Hel's servant. It's magical and can change shape to be whatever Hel needs it to be. It could be a group of people, a horse, some birds, a building. But it's always black and sticky. Keep away from it – it feeds on Viking spirits. Let it touch you for too long and there will be nothing left of you.'

Whetstone shuddered. He glanced over his shoulder as if he was expecting a sticky, black creature to be standing just behind him.

Lotta straightened her armour. 'Right. Let's track down this Helhest and find out what it did with my shield. C'mon, Whetstone.'

The bridge keeper's head snapped up. 'Whetstone?' He wobbled slightly.

Lotta cringed. She couldn't believe the story of their adventures had reached all the way down to Helheim. Whetstone might be enjoying his newfound fame, but she wasn't. The other Valkyries would never let her live this down. Lotta just hoped the man didn't ask for an autograph; Whetstone would be insufferable.

Whetstone continued to hop from one foot to another, trying to keep his feet out of the snow. 'Let's c-cross the bridge again – it's too c-cold here. I can't think straight.'

The man swallowed. 'One way only,' he explained, his voice croaky. 'Look.'

Whetstone spun round. The bridge was gone. The river

was gone. The green riverbank was gone. Snow covered the land for miles behind them.

'Are you – sure you're all right?' the man asked, peering at Whetstone over the top of his glasses.

'No, I'm half left,' Whetstone replied, goggling at the snow-covered landscape.

The man laughed and patted Whetstone on the shoulder. 'Good one.'

'Now you're at it with the jokes,' Lotta muttered.

'Look, why don't you come inside.' The man gestured towards the golden hut. 'It's warmer in there, and you can tell me what's really going on.'

Whetstone nodded enthusiastically.

Lotta crossed her arms. Whetstone hadn't wanted to hang around when she was trying to contact Asgard, but now he had plenty of time to laze about in golden huts? She didn't know what the man had heard about them, but if he turned out to be some of sort of Whetstone superfan, she didn't think she would be able to cope.

Whetstone looked at Lotta with pleading eyes.

'Fine,' Lotta sighed. 'But we're not staying long.'

'Wait.' Whetstone gave the man's beard a sharp tug.

'What was that for?' he complained.

Whetstone grinned. 'Just checking.' He then tottered on frozen toes towards the sounds of a crackling fire.

❁

A little while later, Whetstone sat wrapped in blankets in the golden hut. A delicious smell wafted from the cauldron over the fire, and the fluffy cat stretched out on a rug, purring. Whetstone watched as the bridge keeper, who said his name was Hod, bustled about, finding bowls and spoons.

The door banged open, filling the air with snowflakes, and in marched Lotta with armfuls of blackened branches. She dumped them on the ground next to the fire. 'There.'

'How are you not cold?' Whetstone shivered and burrowed deeper into his blankets.

'I don't mind the cold. Plus,' she added in a lower voice, 'I'm not human yet. It's different for Valkyries: we're made of pure battle frenzy. It keeps you toasty.' She plopped down next to him and poked at the fire.

'Maybe that's how we'll know when you turn human – you'll start trying to borrow my vest.'

Lotta stuck her tongue out.

Whetstone had been thinking; he nodded towards Hod. 'Do you think we should ask him if he's seen my dad?'

Lotta wrinkled her nose. 'Can we trust him? He works for Hel.'

'You already told him about your shield.' Whetstone pouted. 'Why shouldn't I get some help too?'

'Nice firewood.' Hod joined them by the fire. 'Hey, what's brown and sticky? A stick.'

Lotta groaned.

Hod handed Whetstone and Lotta bowls of something warm and meaty.

'How do you get food here?' Lotta asked, poking a finger into her bowl. 'If everyone is dead, there's no need to grow food.'

The man grinned; several of his teeth were missing. 'You'd be surprised what people have buried with them. Furs, food, weapons. Then they get here and realize it's all worthless. Dead people don't need much. They don't feel the cold, they can't eat and there's no point in fighting any more. They either give their grave goods to me or take them as gifts for Hel, thinking they can win her favour.'

'I guess you've figured out that we're not dead, then,' Whetstone said, gobbling down the stew. Lotta rolled her eyes.

Hod smiled. 'You might have given it away, yes.'

'Are the Lost Things different to grave goods?' Lotta asked.

Hod nodded. 'If something is lost by accident, it joins the Lost Things. If it's sent as part of a funeral, it's grave goods. It doesn't make much difference really. Hel keeps it all.'

Whetstone wiped his mouth with the back of his hand. It was good to have a full belly again. 'What's Hel like?'

Hod looked thoughtful for a moment. 'She's cold, and rich, and –' he paused – 'lonely, I think. Smells pretty bad too. Try to stay upwind of her.'

Whetstone wrinkled his nose in confusion.

'She's half woman, half corpse,' Lotta said through a mouthful of stew.

Whetstone wrinkled his nose further. 'Which bit is—?'

'Does it matter?'

'Listen –' Hod put his bowl down, suddenly serious –

'I don't know how you two came to Helheim, or what you want here—'

Whetstone opened his mouth to reply. Lotta trod on his toe.

'*But*, whatever you're looking for, you won't find it,' Hod continued. 'Once someone – or something – comes to Helheim, it never leaves.'

'Oh yeah? We'll see about that,' Lotta muttered, dropping her spoon back into the bowl.

'The Nine Worlds would be filled with ghosts, otherwise,' Hod continued reasonably. 'Your best bet is to stay here with me. I have food and a fire – you won't last long out there without that.'

Whetstone glanced at Lotta. 'Hod's right, kind of. We need an actual plan. We can't just march up to – Where does Hel live? Hel-hall?'

Hod barked a laugh. 'No, her hall is called Eljudnir. It means, *Sprayed by Snowstorms*.'

'Sounds cosy.' Whetstone huddled into his blankets. 'We can't just walk up to Eggy-jug-nir and ask for the shield and the . . . *other stuff*. There's no way she'd give it to us.'

'Well, we can't just sit around here.' Lotta bit off a piece of her thumbnail and spat it into the fire. 'I've got about a day before . . .' She looked meaningfully at Whetstone.

Whetstone thought for a moment. It wasn't fair that Lotta was taking over their quest to Helheim with her shield problems. Finding his dad and the harp string was way more important. He was the Hero, after all, not her. He made a decision and turned to Hod. 'If you're the bridge keeper, does that mean you see everyone who comes to Helheim?'

Lotta threw up her arms in exasperation.

'The bridge is the only way in. And there is no way out.'

'So, do you ever get anyone coming here who shouldn't be here? Like . . . living people, perhaps?' His voice went all high and peculiar as he spoke.

Lotta raised her eyebrows at him.

'Other than you, you mean?' Hod leaned back. 'Sometimes we get those who are supposed to go to Niflheim trying to get in, but that's as exciting as it gets.'

Whetstone nodded, disappointment sour in his stomach. That must mean that his father was dead. Vali had warned him as much before Loki had turned him to stone. Living people wouldn't last long in a place like this.

'What about Loki? Does he ever come to visit Hel?' Lotta asked.

It was Whetstone's turn to stare at her. She shrugged.

'Not that I've ever seen.'

'But he's a shapeshifter,' Lotta continued. 'He could have been in disguise.'

Hod tapped his glasses. 'Not with these. Nothing can hide from these.'

'What are they?' Whetstone asked, still trying to shake off his disappointment.

Hod took off the glasses and tucked them into his tunic pocket. Without them, his eyes sparkled with life. 'They're magic. It's how I can see who is coming over the bridge. Hel's subjects are usually invisible.'

Whetstone glanced around. A chill crept down his spine. 'You mean we could be surrounded by dead people right now, but I just can't see them?'

Hod laughed. 'Don't worry. You soon get used to it.'

'What are the glasses made of?' Lotta asked.

'Valkyrie tears, they tell me. And you can imagine how difficult they are to find!'

Lotta let out a snort of laughter. Hod got up to tidy the bowls away.

Whetstone leaned towards Lotta. 'Can you see the dead people?' he whispered.

She shook her head. 'I guess I've lost that power too. No transformations, no seeing spirits. What's next?'

'Well, I bet you're still terrible at poetry, so no change there.'

Lotta thumped him on the arm.

Somewhere in the distance came a lone wolf's howl. It rolled around the golden hut, making the metal walls vibrate unpleasantly. Hod spun round, the bowls dropping out of his trembling fingers. 'Hel's on the move – she must know you're here. You need to hide!'

In a moment Whetstone went from being warm, comfortable and full of stew to cold with terror. His skin prickled at the thought of Loki's daughter finding them. He pushed off the blankets and started to pull on as many hairy socks as he could manage before wedging his feet into a pair of sturdy boots. If he was going to be captured, he was not going to be cold.

Hod threw baskets and clothes across the room, revealing a large, charred trunk. He lifted the lid. 'Get inside. They know me, but if they find you . . .'

Whetstone paused while pulling three tunics over his head. 'I'm not getting in there.' His head popped out of the tunics. 'Last time I was shut in a chest, I was almost eaten by Jormungandr.'

Lotta rolled her eyes. 'Oh, for Odin's sake.' She clambered into the chest. 'You're going to have to get over that.'

Hod closed the lid and covered it with a rug.

Whetstone slid under a narrow bench, tucking himself into the shadows, his heart pounding. Hod tipped a cup of water over the fire, plunging the room into darkness. The fireplace hissed, dark smoke curling out.

Red sunlight spilt into the room as the door creaked open. Something *big* sniffed the air.

'Hey, Fenrir,' Hod said, holding the door. 'Good to see you. Do you want to hear a joke?'

That was Fenrir? Loki's son? Whetstone eased his head towards the doorway to check.

'What do you call a really cold dog? A pupsicle!'

With a panting laugh, the wolf stepped inside, his claws clicking against the golden floor. Whetstone held his breath, praying that Fenrir wouldn't notice him. Or Lotta. A black nose the size of man's fist thrust itself under the bench and sniffed. The boy tried to shrink away, but sharp teeth fastened

123

round his leg and wrenched him out. His fingers scraped helplessly against the smooth floor.

A grey wolf as big as a bear filled the room. Black eyes stared down at the boy on the floor. The wolf's muzzle wrinkled, a growl rumbling out. Whetstone lurched away, bashing into the trunk where Lotta lay hiding. The trunk flew open, revealing the Valkyrie, tangled in fabric. With difficulty, she freed herself and drew her rusty sword.

Hod stepped forward, waving his hands. 'Come on, Fenrir. They're just kids! There's no need for Hel to find out about this.'

The light dimmed as another figure stepped through the doorway: a woman dressed head to toe in black, a scarf wrapped over her hair and covering the lower half of her face, her eyes hidden deep in their sockets.

Hod stumbled backwards, his eyes wide with fear.

The creature pulled the scarf away from her face, revealing a series of needle-like teeth set in a skeleton jaw.

Whetstone stared, horror-struck. She was more terrifying than the wolf. The top half of her face was still human; the bottom a skull.

'There is nothing you can hide from me, old man,' Hel rasped.

With that, the golden room filled with shadows, blotting out what little light there was and surging over Whetstone and Lotta like a tide. Whetstone gasped. The Helhest was so cold that it almost burned. Remembering what Hod had said about it eating spirits, Whetstone desperately tried to free himself. Sticky tendrils wrapped tightly around him, pinning his arms to his sides before dragging him out of the hut.

Outside in the snow stood a sledge drawn by three misshapen horses. Whetstone was dumped, gasping, in the

back, followed promptly by Lotta. His skin stung where the Helhest had grabbed him. The Helhest surged over the sledge and around them, forming a cage. It gleamed in the sunlight, shades of green and blue appearing in its depths.

Lotta threw herself at the bars. 'Let me out!' She recoiled, her hands covered in strings of black slime.

Hod appeared behind Whetstone, peering through the bars. 'Don't panic. I'll follow you to the Great Hall when I can. Take this.' He thrust a leather pouch through the bars and into Whetstone's hands.

The woman swung herself into the driver's seat.

'Please bring the cat!' Lotta yelled as the sledge lurched away, dragged over the snow by the crooked horses. The red sun beamed down on them with a light that had no warmth.

Hod's voice drifted after them. 'Hey, what's a cat's favourite colour? Purr-ple!'

Whetstone grimaced at the joke.

Lotta wrapped her arms round herself and shivered. Whetstone realized that her powers must already be fading. He shrugged out of one of his many cloaks. 'Take this.' The sledge jolted, bearing them across Helheim and towards the Great Hall.

Chapter Eleven

Road to Hel

The sledge drew to a stop at the foot of a flat-topped mountain. Near-vertical walls of dry, brown stone towered over them. With a quiet, slithering noise that made all the hairs on the back of Whetstone's neck stand up, the Hel-hest cage dissolved, the inky strands vanishing into the shadows under the cart.

Hel swung herself out of the driver's seat and stalked round to face Whetstone and Lotta. 'Out.'

Whetstone jumped down, his eyes fixed on a twisting path that led up the side of the mountain. The woman shoved his shoulder and they started the long trudge to the top. As they climbed, the landscape changed, endless winter giving way to dusty, brown rocks. A blustery wind whipped soil into twisting shapes and the sun grew stronger. It wasn't warm exactly, but it wasn't cold either. Behind him, Whetstone could hear Lotta breathing heavily and the crunch of Fenrir's paws on the dry ground. The boy bundled up the extra cloaks in his arms, and his feet started to sweat inside their many socks.

He rounded the top of the mountain, a stitch in his side and his breath coming in short gasps. A flat, empty landscape opened up in front of him. In the distance sat the crouching shape of a Great Hall. The hall's roof was black, heavily thatched and so low it almost reached the ground. It did not look like the type of place you would find roaring fires and toasted marshmallows.

Whetstone longed for a tree or a hint of birdsong. Even Bragi's annoying face would make everything a bit more normal. He glanced at Lotta with a pang of concern – her jaw was tight and her hands curled into fists. Maybe the shield thing was a bit more important than he'd realized. He tried to give her an encouraging smile as they plodded onwards.

Whetstone fixed his eyes on the grey boulder that lay directly in their path. His footsteps quickened. Boulders were normal: you found them everywhere. He raised a hand to brush his fingertips against the rough surface. For a second, Whetstone could almost imagine he was back in Krud.

'Don't even think about touching me with your thieving hands,' said the boulder.

Whetstone stumbled back in surprise. The boulder shifted and slowly got to its feet, revealing itself to be not a boulder, but a tall, pale-skinned boy with dark rings round his eyes.

'Vali?'

The boy pulled a knife out of his belt and twisted it between his fingers. He had always been fond of sharp blades. Whetstone swallowed. They hadn't exactly parted on the best of terms.

'I told you he was a Troll,' Lotta muttered.

Whetstone stared at the taller boy. 'But the sun's out! You're moving around and everything – surely you should turn to stone?'

Vali shook back his dark hair, which, now that Whetstone looked at it properly, he realized was streaked with moss. 'Those rules only apply on Midgard.' Despite Loki's spell, Vali had retained most of his good looks, but his clothes and skin were now shades of grey and there was a sheen to his face like a freshly washed pebble.

'Ah.' Whetstone gulped. 'Is that why you came to Helheim?'

Vali gave a half-smile. 'I wanted a change of scenery.'

Whetstone looked around. 'And this is better than Krud?'

Vali's face froze. 'It has better *company*.'

'Oh.' Whetstone rubbed his neck. 'So, Hel must be your sister?'

'Half-sister.'

Whetstone nodded hurriedly. Fenrir panted a laugh.

Lotta shouldered forward. 'My shield, have you seen it?'

Vali's face cracked into a smile. It looked strange on his face, as if it wasn't used to being there.

'Enough talk,' rasped Hel, tugging down her mask to reveal her pointed teeth. 'Keep walking.'

'I think I'll come with you.' Vali tucked the knife back into his belt. 'I could do with a laugh.'

The woman hissed between her teeth, but said nothing. She gave Whetstone a shove and he stumbled onwards, leading them in a silent procession towards the Great Hall.

Unlike the Great Halls in Asgard, this one didn't have steps leading up to a brightly painted front door. It wasn't even sitting level with the ground like the Great Hall in Krud. Instead the door was half buried in the ground with worn steps leading down to it. Fenrir sat down beside the steps and panted, his red tongue lolling.

Whetstone hesitated at the top step.

Hel leaned close to his ear. 'What are you waiting for?'

Whetstone tried not to shudder at those teeth being so near to his face.

The door swung open as he descended. Screwing up his courage and trying not to think about what might be inside, Whetstone took a deep breath, and stepped into the Hall.

The steps descended about as far as the height of a man,

leading into a huge cave-like room. Light came from tiny windows high in the roof, which only manged to turn the darkness into shadows. Strange misshapen heaps appeared in the gloom. Whetstone blinked, waiting for his eyes to adjust.

Hel clapped her hands and tall white candles flickered to life, forming pools of brightness. Whetstone stared. The room was vast, it was impressive and it was full of junk. Lost Things and grave goods were heaped against distant walls. Long polished tables rose out of the mess like wooden islands, empty benches bobbing on either side.

Behind him, Lotta caught her breath. 'I was expecting it to be at least a *bit* like Valhalla.'

Whetstone crept forward, his foot catching a bronze arm ring, which skittered across the floor. 'Do you think there are people on those benches?'

'I can't see anyone.'

'That doesn't mean they're not there.' Whetstone suppressed a shudder.

At one end of the hall was a low platform with the top table and a range of ornate chairs. These were the seats reserved for the most important guests. Whetstone stopped in front of them.

Hel pushed forward, unwinding her long scarf from round her head. Half her hair was a glossy black, the other half as white and fine as cobwebs. She stepped up on to the low platform, unbuckling her cloak and dropping it to the floor to reveal a short-sleeved tunic and dark trousers. She lowered herself on to the most ornate chair, which sat in the centre. White and spindly, it looked like spiderweb turned to marble.

Whetstone tried not to stare. One of the woman's arms was pink and human, the other nothing but bones. She moved her hand, the small bones in her wrist clicking together in a strangely fascinating way. Half woman, half corpse, just as Lotta had said. Whetstone felt his skin creep. Hel watched them expectantly.

Whetstone's eyes flicked sideways to Lotta, wondering how they were going to explain their arrival in Helheim. But Lotta had her eyes fixed on an object behind Hel's head.

'That's my SHIELD!' Lotta strode forward, her boots kicking up sparks against the flagstone floor. She pointed a finger at the wall behind Hel's throne. Hanging there between a faded tapestry and a twisted sword was a round wooden shield split into six segments, each faintly glowing in a different colour. 'I need it BACK.'

Hel's eyes creased like she was smiling. 'This is the Land of the Lost. Once something or someone makes its way here, they are beyond finding.'

'Well, I've found it,' Lotta announced, placing her foot on the platform.

'But you can't *take* it, can you? Not now I've claimed it,' Hel hissed, her voice suddenly vicious.

Lotta froze, her boot stuck to the platform. 'I can't move,' she whispered through gritted teeth.

'I have all the power here, little girl. The shield is mine, and the only way to get it back is if I return it to you. Which I won't.'

Lotta grimaced and with a huge effort pulled her foot free. Hel smirked. Whetstone glanced over his shoulder to see Vali snigger as he played with another knife.

'Besides, the magic from this shield increases my own power.' Hel picked up a shiny red apple from a bowl beside her chair. It withered and turned black in her hand. 'A few more of these and I'll have the magic I need to leave Helheim.'

'Odin will never let you out,' Lotta panted. 'He banished you here and he can keep you here.'

'You sound very sure of that, but things are changing in Asgard. New friends are rising and soon not even Odin will be able to stand in our way.'

Lotta ground her teeth.

Whetstone stepped forward with his palms raised. 'Look, let's all calm down. Just give us the shield and we'll get out of your hair . . . bones . . . whatever.'

'That's the trouble with you,' said Vali. 'You're always taking things that don't belong to you.'

Hel giggled. 'Oh yes, *Whetstone*. Yes: I know who you are. And, no: you're not going anywhere.' Despite her raspy voice, she suddenly sounded much younger. She pulled a polished comb made of antler out of her hair. 'This Lost Thing arrived yesterday.' Several lines of runes were carved into the comb. As Hel read them aloud, Whetstone's heart sank.

Whetstone has the riddle I need.
Don't let him get away. L

'Daddy doesn't often send me messages –' Hel stuck the comb back into her hair – 'so it must be important.' Hel fixed her eyes on Whetstone. 'So, Whetstone-with-the-riddle, Whetstone-don't-let-him-get-away.' Hel giggled again, the creepiest giggle Whetstone had ever heard. The type of giggle a little girl would make while chopping off the heads of her teddy bears. 'What is the riddle?'

Whetstone gulped. 'No idea! That must be about a totally different Whetstone.' His eyes slipped sideways to Vali. The knife had stilled in his fingers.

Hel leaned back in her chair. 'I think Daddy would be very interested to know that you're in Helheim.' She tapped her skeleton jaw in thought. 'Maybe I should tell him.'

'I wouldn't do that,' Whetstone gabbled. 'It would be a total waste of his time. We're only here because Lotta needs her shield back.' Sweat prickled between his shoulder blades. 'Once we've got that, we'll be off.'

Vali barked a laugh. The sound echoed around the hall.

Lotta was practically vibrating in frustration. 'That shield is MINE! GIVE IT BACK!'

Hel picked at her trousers. 'Your friends need to learn some manners, little brother.'

Vali glared, his face pale in the darkness. For one uncomfortable moment, he reminded Whetstone of Loki.

'They are not my friends,' the boy spat, making Whetstone flinch. The knife spun out of his fingers and landed point down next to Hel's foot. 'And I am not your little brother.'

Hel's eyes narrowed. 'Behave yourself, Vali, or I'll tell Daddy on you. Just think – when I give him these two, I'll be his favourite, not you.' She kicked Vali's knife away. As she moved, Whetstone caught a glimpse of blue-black flesh, and the scent of death filled his nostrils. He tried not to gag.

'His favourite?' Vali scoffed. 'How often has Father been to visit you here, in your kingdom, which you're soooooo proud of? Oh that's right – never!'

'You're just jealous,' Hel spat.

Vali stopped laughing. 'At least I didn't get banished from Asgard.'

'At least I'm still half human!'

'At least I don't have cobwebs for hair.'

'At least *my mum* isn't ashamed of me, stone boy!'

A sheen covered Vali's face; his jaw clenched. 'At least I know *why* Father wants the riddle.'

Whetstone bit his lip. This was some messed up sibling rivalry.

Hel's face creased in a scowl. 'Whatever comes to my land is mine. You, and you, and you.' She stabbed a bony finger at each of them in turn. 'You all belong to me. I am the Keeper of the Lost and the Queen of the Dead. No one and nothing can leave my realm without my say-so. You *will* give me the riddle, you *will* tell me why Daddy wants it and I am *never* giving back the shield. Never, ever, ever, ever.' Hel crossed her arms and stuck her nose in the air. 'So there.'

Lotta shook with fury – well, either fury or frustration – her brown eyes fixed on her shield.

Whetstone shuddered. There was no way he was staying here with this power-mad zombie woman. He had to find his dad and the harp string and get out of here. Oh, and get Lotta's shield, of course. But how? Hel knew who they were, so there was no way she was just going to let them walk out. They would have to escape, or – a thought popped into Whetstone's head – win their freedom. Hel *was* Loki's daughter after all.

136

Whetstone cleared his throat. 'So you don't want to make this *interesting*, then?'

Lotta stopped shaking and tore her eyes away from her shield. 'What?'

'How about— a contest?'

Hel leaned forward, resting her spindly elbow on the arm of her throne and cupping her jaw in her hand. The candles flickered. 'What sort of contest?'

'A . . . game?' Whetstone improvised. 'For our freedom.' He could feel Lotta's eyes boring into the side of his face.

'What are you doing?' she hissed.

Hel twisted her white hair round a bony finger. 'I like games.'

'It's a trick,' said Vali flatly. 'It always is with Whetstone.'

'Be quiet, Vali.' Hel smoothed back her two-tone hair. 'No one is listening to you.'

'I was trying to be nice,' said Vali, walking backwards away from his sister. 'No one can say I didn't try to stop you.'

'I'm not listening to you, little brother.'

'I'm OLDER than you!'

'I'm BETTER than you!'

'Oh yeah?'

Whetstone leaned closer to Lotta. 'Should we just go . . . ?'

'GET OUT OF MY HALL!' Hel bellowed, making them all jump, her face pale with anger. She pointed a finger at Vali.

Vali backed away. 'I wouldn't want to be in your hall. It stinks, and you stink, and this whole place is stupid!'

137

Hel picked up Vali's knife from where it had been left by her throne. She hurled it across the room. It flew through the air, trailing green sparks. 'SHUT UP!'

Whetstone stepped forward. 'As fun as this is, maybe we should focus on the contest.' Hel snapped her head back towards him, her needle teeth snarling. Whetstone tried to keep his eyes on the top half of her face. 'What sort of game do you fancy? Charades? Hide-and-seek? I spy? Lotta is really good at poetry.' Lotta aimed a kick at him.

'*It's a trap,*' Vali called in a sing-song voice as he picked up the knife.

'I DON'T NEED YOUR HELP!' Hel bellowed, pummelling her fists on her throne. 'GET OUT!'

Vali sat down on a bench, his back towards his sister.

Whetstone waved his hands, trying to attract her attention

again. 'So, the contest. If we win, we get to leave, with the shield and the answer to any question we want to ask.'

Hel's eyes narrowed with suspicion. 'Any *question*?'

'What?' Whetstone opened his eyes innocently. 'Isn't that something Heroes traditionally get in the Sagas?'

Hel sniffed. 'And when you lose?'

'We'll give you the riddle,' Lotta answered, her eyes bright.

'What?' Whetstone made a grab for Lotta's arm, but she ducked away. There was no way they could give Hel the riddle. Whetstone's heart thumped loudly.

'Yeah, I bet your dad would love it if you could give him the riddle.' Lotta skipped away from Whetstone, her skin glowing copper in the candlelight. 'As spoken by the magic cup of Chief Awfulrick.' Lotta waggled her eyebrows at Whetstone like she was trying to tell him something. But whatever message she was trying to send, Whetstone wasn't receiving.

Hel sucked in a breath. 'The riddle?'

'Yes. Vali might know why Loki wants it, but he doesn't know what it is.'

Hel squinted at Vali, who ignored her.

'Loki would be so impressed. It's what he really wants, after all. He doesn't care about having Whetstone as long as he has the riddle.'

'Lotta, you cannot be serious,' Whetstone muttered, grabbing her arm.

'We have to offer her something – I *need* my shield,' Lotta growled.

Whetstone turned back to Hel. 'We'll give you something else instead. I know where we can find a scrying bowl – or how about a big fluffy cat? It could keep you company?'

'We're not giving her the cat!' Lotta hissed.

'I don't want a stupid cat – I want the riddle!' Hel thumped the arm of her throne.

'You can't have the riddle!' Whetstone yelled.

'Then you can't have the shield!' Hel yelled back.

'I NEED MY SHIELD!' Lotta bellowed.

'*Your* shield?' Hel snarled. 'You mean, *my* shield.'

'It's a trick,' Vali called out again.

'SHUT UP, VALI!'

Hel sat back in her throne breathing heavily. She jiggled her leg, sending the scent of decay wafting into the room. Whetstone tried not to breathe through his nose.

Hel took a deep breath. 'OK. It's a deal.' She narrowed her eyes at Whetstone. 'The riddle versus the shield and one question.' She held up a single finger as emphasis.

Lotta nodded enthusiastically. Whetstone felt his heart sink.

'And, just so you know, we have a special place in Helheim for oath-breakers.'

'Is it a nice place?'

'Only if you really like snakes.'

Lotta nodded. 'Fair enough. But no telling Loki we're here.' She put her hands on her hips. 'Not until the contest is over. This is us against you. No outsiders.' She held out her hand for Hel to shake. Whetstone cringed at the sight of Hel's

140

bony fingers touching Lotta's skin and stuck his own hands in his pockets.

'I'll show you the games we play in Helheim.' Hel smiled. 'Follow me.' She swept from the platform and towards the main doors, her nose in the air as she passed Vali.

Chapter Twelve

The Race

Outside, the red sun filled the land with dusky shadows. Fenrir lifted his muzzle and sniffed as Whetstone and Lotta followed Hel a short distance away from the hall.

'Why did you tell her we'd give her the riddle?' Whetstone hissed. 'We went to all that effort to stop Loki getting it – now you want to just give it away!'

'I'm not giving it to him – and why did you have to offer her a deal?' Lotta hissed back. 'Didn't you learn your lesson last time? Anyway, I have it all under control. The longer we keep her distracted, the less chance she has of contacting Loki. When I get my shield back, I'll be able to transform properly, and I'll get us out before he even knows we're here.'

'We can't go until I've found the . . . you-know-what,' Whetstone muttered. 'Although I'm not so sure we're in the right place. My dad is supposed to still be alive, but Hod said there weren't any living people here.'

'Well, you can ask Hel about that with your *one question*, can't you?'

Hel turned to face them, sandy soil staining the bottom of

her trousers. 'The challenge is a race. Beat my champion and you win.' She dragged a toe through the dust. 'This is the start and finish line. The race is three times around the Great Hall.'

Lotta nodded. 'Are we using horses or chariots or—?'

'Nothing. This is a foot race. You must both run.'

Whetstone grabbed Lotta's arm and drew her a few steps away. 'Sounds simple enough. Are you any good at running? You know, without your Valkyrie powers?'

'I'm turning human – my legs aren't falling off.' Lotta started unbuckling her armour, dumping her breastplate and wrist guards on the ground. 'I'll run as fast as the wind if it means I get my shield back.'

Whetstone nodded. 'This'll be easy! Dead people can't be that fast, and I'm brilliant at running away from things. We'll have the shield back in no time. I wonder who we're racing against?'

Hel giggled and beckoned something over. Whetstone turned to see a shadow pass through the doorway of the Great Hall. The shadow formed into a tall boy.

Whetstone smirked. 'Vali? He's made of stone. There's no way he could beat us in a race.'

Vali stepped to one side, but the shadow continued to pour out. Huge and black, it shimmered faintly, draining what little colour there was in the place.

Lotta stood up. 'Not that stuff again.'

The Helhest broke away from the hall, slithering across the ground like a mass of glistening beetles. Lotta skipped out of the way as it approached, trying to stop it touching her feet. It

143

slid over their shadows, and when it moved on, it left part of itself behind. Whetstone lifted an arm, watching as the inky shape infected his own shadow in the same disturbing way.

'We've got Helhest shadows.' Lotta scrunched up her nose, disgusted.

'What is she playing at?' Whetstone wondered aloud.

The remainder of the Helhest swarmed towards Hel, where it swelled upwards to form a group of women in short skirts holding pom-poms – like cheerleaders after an accident in a tar factory.

Lotta's lip curled. 'Who are *they*?'

'My supporters. The Hel's Belles.'

The figures leaped around, performing athletic kicks and jumps. They shook their pom poms and cheered:

> *Give us an L!*
>> *Give us an O!*
>>> *Give us a K!*
>>>> *Give us an I!*
>>>>> *TEAM LOKI!*

Whetstone wrinkled his nose. 'Loki has a team? He's like the opposite of team.'

Hel tossed her hair. 'Three times round the Great Hall, beating my Helhest. Or you could just give me the riddle now?'

Whetstone shaded his eyes to look at the sun. He made a few calculations. 'But if this is the finish line, and the Helhest is in our shadows, the sun will be behind us, so our shadows will always cross the line first.'

Hel giggled again. Even Vali looked as if he was trying not to smirk.

'Maybe we could wait till later?'

'No time passes in Helheim, so the sun doesn't move here,' Lotta hissed. She marched up to Hel. 'Why should we run if we know we're going to lose?'

'Oh, you'll run,' replied Hel. She stuck her bone fingers in her mouth and gave a piercing whistle. Fenrir, the enormous wolf, pricked up his ears and replied with a bark that made all their heads ring.

Whetstone took a swift step behind Lotta. 'You have a pet wolf-dog-thing. You can deal with him.'

'He's nothing like Broken Tooth,' Lotta replied, shoving Whetstone away. Broken Tooth was the name of her very soppy dog back in Asgard. 'Anyway, you grew up in a foster home for wolves – this should be right up your alley.'

'Yes, and they used to try to eat me.' After his parents had been taken by the cursed harp strings, Whetstone had been brought up by his foster mother, Angrboda (or as Whetstone called her – the Angry Bogey), a surprisingly tall and bony woman who ran a home for abandoned wolf cubs. None of the Angry Bogey's wolves had looked anything like this one.

Fenrir padded over to Hel, who stroked his head. A low rumble came from the wolf's throat. Ironically, the sound made Whetstone want to run very fast indeed. Away from the wolf. He gazed up into the empty sky to avoid looking at Fenrir's long teeth.

'If you don't run, Fenrir will eat you,' Hel said simply. Fenrir fixed them with a stare, opening his mouth to reveal his pointed teeth.

'So, it's three times round the Great Hall, trying to beat our own shadows.' Lotta rubbed her neck. 'Or we get eaten by the wolf. If we win, I get my shield. If we lose, I have to give you the riddle?' There was a wobble in her voice and she didn't look half as confident as she had in the hall.

'And I have witnesses,' Hel preened. 'Everybody's watching.'

Whetstone looked around the empty field. It was hard not to imagine thousands of invisible spectators, silently watching them. Lotta shivered, clearly having the same thought. Whetstone mouthed, '*You OK?*' The Valkyrie nodded.

Hel's cheerleaders bounced acrobatically behind their queen, performing flips and high kicks. Hel clapped her hands and several of the cheerleaders glooped together to form a perfect replica of her throne. Hel settled back in her chair.

Moving to the start line, Whetstone racked his brains for something, anything, that could help them. There had to be something he could do. He might be a prisoner in the Land of

146

Lost Things with only a poorly Valkyrie for company, but that didn't mean he had to give up. He was a Hero after all.

He slowly pulled off his spare tunics and all but one pair of hairy socks, trying to buy time before the race started. Feeling a bump in one of the pockets, Whetstone drew out the pouch Hod had given to him. The leather was smooth and well-worn and something lumpy lay inside it. Whetstone left it on top of his pile of clothes. Whatever it was, it would have to wait until after the race.

He pulled his boots back on and performed a few stretches, his Helhest-infected shadow copying his movements. An idea started to form.

'How are you so calm? This is impossible,' Lotta groaned, smoothing back her black curls. 'I wonder how bad the place with snakes is?'

'Don't worry,' said Whetstone, still eyeing the Helhest's movements in his shadow. 'I've got an idea. I am a Hero, remember?'

'Oh *good.*'

'When have I ever let you down?' Whetstone turned to look at her with a bit of a grin on his face.

'Do you want a list?' Lotta's mouth screwed up into a squiggle. She lowered herself into a crouch.

'Just run,' Whetstone muttered out of the corner of his mouth, 'and do exactly what I tell you.' The boy sank down, his fingertips digging into the dry, dusty soil. 'How do we know when to start?' he called.

Hel waved a hand dismissively. 'Start when you like. The sooner you start, the sooner you lose.'

Behind them the wolf barked, his voice echoing across the empty landscape.

'Run?' Lotta suggested. Whetstone nodded. Together they darted away from the start line, their feet sending up clouds of dust.

'And they're off!' Hel cackled, her voice bouncing around the field.

The walls of Hel's sunken Great Hall stretched out endlessly. It was more like running around an entire village than a single building. Whetstone's boots thudded into the ground, sending shockwaves up his legs. He slowed to a jog –

148

there was no way he could sprint round the whole thing without dying.

'Fenrir isn't following us,' Lotta panted.

'He doesn't need to. We're running.'

They rounded the first corner, their shadows vanishing as they were swallowed by the larger shadow of the Great Hall.

'What's the plan?' Lotta gasped, her arms pumping.

'For now, just run.'

They rounded the second corner, their shadows separating from the darkness and reappearing behind them. 'If only the finish line was on this side,' Lotta moaned.

They pounded on, their feet leaving tracks in the untouched soil. Breathlessly they turned the last two corners and sped towards the finish line. Vali watched them, his eyes glittering from the doorway.

'One!' Hel called as they passed her throne. 'Two more to go.' The Hel's Belles waved their pom-poms and cheered.

The dry air caught in Whetstone's throat; he swallowed down a mouthful of dust and thought longingly of water. Two more laps. They pounded up the long walls, following their own footsteps. As their shadows vanished again, Lotta looked at him questioningly.

'Tell you next time.'

On and on they ran, Whetstone's breath burning in his chest and a stitch knotting in his side. Lotta's face had look of grim determination, but her feet started to stumble over the flat ground. Whetstone slowed to keep pace with her.

'Two!' Hel cried as they passed her, the cheerleaders

performing a series of backflips. 'I hope you're not getting tired. Fenrir – after them!' The wolf licked his lips and loped away from Hel, his long legs eating up the ground. Faint, lilting music filled the air. One of the ghosts must be giving them a musical accompaniment, Whetstone supposed.

Whetstone could hear Fenrir's feet crunching behind them. He sped up. 'Come on – last lap.'

Lotta nodded, her feet struggling to lift clear of the ground. She started to drop behind. Whetstone grabbed her arm and dragged her onwards, her brown skin cold and clammy.

'Keep going. We don't win if you get eaten,' he said encouragingly.

Passing through the shadow of the Great Hall again, Whetstone puffed, 'Run when I say run, and stop when I say stop.'

Lotta raised her eyebrows. 'That's it? *Genius*.'

Whetstone nodded, too breathless for more words.

They turned the corner and headed down the third wall, the grey wolf getting closer with every step. Whetstone slowed, the pain from his side intense. Behind them, Fenrir gave a loud yip.

Staggering and bumping into each other, they passed the third corner. Whetstone glanced at the Helhest glinting in their shadows, biding its time. He crossed his fingers, hoping that this would work.

Lotta waggled her eyebrows as they rounded the last corner, her breath coming fast and shallow. The boy winked. The finish line lay ahead of them. Their shadows twitched, starting to move with their own power, stretching out dark fingers to cross the line first.

'Stop!' Whetstone yelled. Lotta stumbled to a halt, breathing heavily.

'Keep running!' Hel screamed, standing up on her throne, which grew larger, lifting her up into the dead sky.

Lotta jogged a couple of steps as Whetstone sped up to take the lead, his Helhest-filled shadow reaching out its arms to touch the finish line.

'Now RUN!' he yelled back at Lotta.

Lotta screwed up her face. With a loud *pop*, wings materialized out of her back. Fenrir sneezed as the feathers tickled his nose. Flapping her wings, the Valkyrie shot forward, her toes weaving across the racecourse, her eyes fixed on the finish line. As she overtook him, Whetstone stepped sideways so their shadows crossed. Now it looked as if Lotta was going to win. All the Helhest surged out of Whetstone's shadow, creeping across the dry ground to join Lotta's.

'STOP!' Whetstone bellowed.

Lotta locked her feet together and flattened her wings. Her shadow a hair's breadth from the line Hel had drawn in the sand. The Valkyrie collapsed backwards, throwing a cloud of feathers into the air and pulling her shadow away from the finish line. Fenrir loomed over her, drool dripping on to her face.

Whetstone shot forward like a rocket, he and his uninfected shadow crossing the finish line in a sprint. He staggered to a stop and dropped to his hands and knees, gasping for air, his heart pounding as if it was about to leap out of his chest. Peering through his legs, he saw the wolf growl at Lotta before slouching away.

'Did it work?' Lotta wheezed.

Whetstone looked round to check his shadow: it looked normal. But something the colour of jet was oozing out of Lotta's. The defeated Helhest crawled away, vanishing into the shadows of the Great Hall. Vali took a step out of the doorway, a smirk on his stony face. It might have been Whetstone's imagination, but he thought he heard the rustle of ghostly voices congratulating him.

Happiness fizzed inside Whetstone's chest. He was right – this had been easy! They had won the shield, and Hel wasn't getting the riddle! He was *good* at this Hero stuff.

Hel thumped her hands on the arms of her throne. 'No! NO! NO!' All around her, the Hel's Belles exploded, as though detonated by an invisible force, coating the landscape in sticky shadows.

Vali ran his hand over his dark hair, wiping off bits of splattered cheerleader. 'I told you so.'

Hel turned on him, her face pink. 'SHUT UP!'

Whetstone got to his feet, clutching his side. 'We did it – we won.'

'Yeah.' Lotta rolled to her feet and staggered forward, one wing stuck out at a funny angle. 'We won.' Swaying slightly, she scraped a lump of Helhest off her cheek and looked up at the woman on her towering throne. 'Now, give me back my shield.'

'And don't forget you have to answer my question,' Whetstone added.

'But the contest isn't over yet,' Hel replied. She pointed a finger at Lotta. 'She didn't finish.'

From the doorway, Vali laughed. The ghostly voices whispered again.

Whetstone goggled at Hel. 'But . . . we both ran. No one said anything about finishing!'

'This is not what we agreed!' Lotta stamped her foot. 'Whetstone crossed the line – that *was* the contest!'

'I don't think so.' Hel ran her hands over her two-tone hair in a gesture that reminded Whetstone of Vali. 'This contest is invalid. We'll have to try again – something different his time.'

'You broke your word,' Whetstone spluttered, his cheeks pink. 'What about the thing with the snakes?'

Hel shrugged. 'I like snakes.' The Helhest throne melted away, lowering the Queen of the Dead to the floor before rejoining the shadows around the Great Hall.

Lotta ground her teeth. A dozen feathers dropped out of one wing. 'What's the next contest? We beat you once – we can do it again.' She marched up to Hel. 'And, this time, no cheating. Whoever wins keeps the shield.'

'Oh, I'll be keeping it all right,' Hel agreed. 'The second challenge will be tomorrow. Until then you are welcome to rest in the Great Hall – with the rest of my subjects,' she added with smirk.

Whetstone crossed his arms, anger burning in his chest. 'No way! I'm not going back into that rubbish dump. You're a cheat and a liar.'

Hel glowered. 'Fine. Stay out here, then. See if I care. But, if you don't compete tomorrow, the shield is definitely mine!'

Lotta's wings gave a final flicker and vanished. She tumbled forward as her knees gave way. In a panic, Whetstone crouched next to her.

'Has it got colder suddenly?' the girl muttered, trying to push herself up. Hel giggled.

An icy dart ran through Whetstone's stomach, overpowering his anger. The run must've used up a lot of Lotta's powers. Whetstone glanced at the sky. The sun still hadn't moved. 'How will we know when it's tomorrow?' he called as Hel returned to the Great Hall.

'When I say so, of course,' Hel replied with a toss of her dead hair.

Chapter Thirteen

Winners and Losers

Whetstone watched Hel and her shadows vanish into the Great Hall. He got to his feet, fear and anger twisting inside him. Lotta groaned, goosebumps rising on her arms as she pushed herself into a sitting position.

'Don't try to move.' Whetstone grabbed a couple of cloaks from where he'd dumped them before the race, and the leather pouch tumbled to the ground. 'These'll help.' He draped them over her.

The enormous grey wolf padded over, sniffing.

'Get away from her. Go on!' Whetstone waved his arms, trying to shoo the beast away.

'Leave him alone. He's only a puppy.' Vali stepped out of the shadows. 'He won't hurt you. Not on purpose.'

'Yeah, that's easy for you to say,' Whetstone muttered, eyeing the wolf as it licked its lips.

'I cannot believe you thought Hel would keep her word.' Vali tutted, his skin glittering like quartz. 'I didn't think even you were that thick.'

'If she tries to trick us again tomorrow, I'm going to poke

her in the t-teeth with my s-sword,' Lotta grunted, her fingers scrabbling in the earth for her scabbard.

'I'd like to see that.' Vali grinned, his own teeth pearly white. 'But it won't happen. You'll lose and be stuck here forever.'

'N-no we w-wont,' Lotta chattered. 'Tomorrow w-we get the shield and th-then w-we'll go.' She shivered and dragged the cloaks in closer with shaking fingers. 'Do you always feel this c-cold?' she asked Whetstone. 'I always th-thought humans were being melodramatic with their fur-lined vests and woolly socks.'

Vali sighed. 'There are three problems with your plan. One: she'll never let you win, not after you beat her today.'

'W-we'll figure something out.'

Vali pulled out a knife. 'Two: even if you do get the shield back, there's no way to leave Helheim.' Beside him Fenrir sat on his haunches, his tongue lolling out like a blood-red flag.

'I'll be able to transform again,' Lotta mumbled. 'I'll fly us out.'

'And three: whatever she promised, she's going to tell Father you're here.' The knife flashed between Vali's fingers. 'She only cares about making Father happy and she knows that giving you to him would make him *very happy*.'

'Anyone would think that you were j-jealous, Vali,' Lotta muttered.

Whetstone swallowed, his throat dry and tight. He wasn't surprised by Vali's words, but he still had to finish the quest. He was no closer to finding his father and the harp string than he had been when they arrived. Lotta and her shield problems had slowed everything down, but at least he could use his one question to find out more after they won the second contest.

'Why do you care what happens to us, Vali?' Whetstone snapped. 'Why are you here if it isn't to help Loki and Hel?'

'Why are *you* here?' Vali retorted. 'And don't give me that rubbish about her shield. I know it's something to do with the riddle.'

Whetstone gulped, trying not to break eye contact with Vali. Eventually, the older boy looked away.

'Hel would've found it if there was a magic harp string here somewhere,' Vali muttered. 'You must've got it wrong.'

Whetstone tried not to twitch. He'd had those thoughts himself.

'It doesn't matter anyway.' Vali spun the knife in his hand. 'Hero or not, you'll be desperate to tell Father the riddle when Hel's finished with you.' He walked away, his grey skin vanishing into the shadows, Fenrir at his heels.

Lotta closed her eyes. Whetstone grabbed the rest of their belongings and sank on to the ground next to her. 'Are you sure we can't just sneak in now and take the shield? Hel's already cheated and it would save a lot of bother.'

Lotta shook her head. 'It won't work. I have to win it back honourably. It's a Valkyrie thing.'

'Do *you* think Loki will come?' Whetstone asked, turning the leather pouch over in his hands.

'With our luck, probably.' Lotta opened her eyes again. 'What is that thing?' She nodded at the pouch.

'Hod gave it to me when we were in the cage.' He

157

fumbled with the drawstring before tipping the contents into his palm. 'It's a necklace.' Coloured beads glinted up at him in the red sunlight.

'Why did he give you a necklace?' Lotta tilted her head.

'I don't know,' Whetstone muttered, running his fingers over the beads.

'He's been stuck at the bridge for too long,' Lotta sniffed. 'He's gone potty. You can give it back to him when he brings the cat.'

'Maybe it's a clue.' Whetstone held the necklace up to the sunlight to inspect it. 'There might be something carved into it? Or maybe it forms a map or a compass or something? If my dad is here, Hod must've seen him arrive, so maybe he's trying to tell us something without skull-face figuring it out?' The beads clinked along the thread alongside a strange coin and a tiny model of a fish. 'The riddle said my dad was still living, and in an ice-locked land.'

Lotta shook her head. 'Hod also said he hadn't seen any living humans in Helheim.'

Whetstone pushed the beads along the thread, watching as they slid up and down. 'I wish there was someone else we could ask,' he muttered.

'Maybe your dad is in Niflheim or Jotunheim – they're both icy,' Lotta suggested. 'I really don't think you should pin your hopes on that crazy old man by the bridge.'

Unnoticed by Whetstone or Lotta, a shape detached itself from the shadows. Quietly, it slipped through the sunken door and into the Great Hall.

Hel pushed down her hood and smiled. How silly those children were to let their guard down so easily. Now she knew the riddle was about the boy's father, and that they had travelled here to find him. Hel unbuckled her cloak and dumped it back on to one of the piles of Lost Things. And if he was still *living*, there was only one person in Helheim that could mean.

A giggle escaped between her needle teeth. Loki would be so pleased when he found out she had the boy *and* the answer to the riddle. Hel hugged herself – all she had to do was bring them together.

Hel dropped on to a bench beside her stony brother, who shuffled away. 'Vali . . .'

'No.'

'But you don't know what I'm going to ask.'

'Still no.'

'How do you fancy getting back into Daddy's good books?'

Vali turned to look at her. 'What are you talking about?'

Hel leaned closer. 'I need you to do something for me.'

Vali squinted. 'This sounds like an excuse to get me to do errands for you. No thanks.'

'I'm serious.' Hel put her skeleton hand on his arm. 'I know who those stupid children are looking for.'

Vali shrugged her off. 'You don't know anything.'

Hel's eyes narrowed. 'I have the answer to Daddy's precious riddle – he's here, in Helheim!'

Vali shoved his hand through his moss-streaked hair and sighed. 'Father isn't looking for a person, Hel. He's looking for a— an object.'

Hel jutted out her jaw. 'Maybe this *person* knows where this *object* is? The boy seemed pretty determined to find him.'

Vali sucked his bottom lip.

'Do this favour for me,' Hel said as she skipped away, 'and I'll tell Daddy you were helpful. Or don't and I'll make sure that being made of stone is the least of your problems.'

❦

Whetstone tried to stay awake, but exhaustion overtook him. Wrapped in spare cloaks, he twitched in an uneasy sleep, dreaming of talking bowls, sea monsters and Loki's twisted smile.

Beside him, Lotta sat, glaring at Hel's Great Hall. It might be more uncomfortable out here on the ground, but to go back inside felt like admitting Hel had beaten them. Lotta scratched in the dirt with her fingers. Her shield was so close she could almost reach out and touch it, but it might as well be a million miles away. Lotta shivered despite the many cloaks Whetstone had tucked round her. She was getting weaker. If

160

she didn't get her shield back soon, it would be too late.

Endless questions churned in her head. Had Glinting-Fire really tried to get rid of her because she was friends with Whetstone, or was Freyja wrong? Surely Odin wouldn't have left Asgard if he knew Glinting-Fire was stirring up trouble, but what did Hel mean about Odin not being able to *stand in their way*? Had they done something to him? Loki had mentioned having *friends in high places*. What was that about? And where *was* Scold?

Whetstone jerked in his sleep, muttering something about turnips.

Then Lotta wondered what would happen if Whetstone failed to get the harp strings. Would Odin, if he ever came back again, change his mind about Whetstone being a Hero, and what would that mean for her? All she wanted was to go back to Asgard with her shield. She missed Valhalla, she missed Broken Tooth and she even missed Scold telling her off. Lotta squinted into the red sky as tears tried to spill on to her cheeks. Her vision blurred either from tears or because she was losing the connection with her shield.

The door to the Great Hall creaked open. Lotta stood up, hurriedly wiping her eyes, her legs stiff. 'Is this how humans feel all the time? It's rubbish,' she grumbled, poking Whetstone with her foot. 'Oi, wake up. It's tomorrow.'

Whetstone blinked himself awake. 'Is he here? Is it Loki?'

Lotta shook the dust out of her dark curls. 'Nope. Just his weird offspring.'

'Watch your language!' Hel stalked out of the Great Hall,

the round shield cradled in her arms. Lotta eyed it hungrily. As Hel propped it against her leg, one of the sections flickered and faded.

'I've decided on the next challenge,' she said, tapping her bony fingers on the shield's rim. 'All you have to do is get the shield away from Fenrir.' The enormous wolf squeezed his way out of the Great Hall, leaving dog hair stuck in the doorframe.

Whetstone shoved the leather pouch into his pocket and gestured at Vali as he sloped round the corner of the building. 'Where's he going?'

Hel smiled, although with her skeleton face it was impossible for her to do anything else. 'My dear brother is just doing a little job for me – that's all.' Vali's footsteps crunched into the distance.

Hel clicked her fingers. Two dark shapes somewhere between crows and tattered flags detached themselves from the shadowy Helhest and swooped down, landing at her feet. The tattered birds picked up the shield and flapped across the empty landscape, Fenrir bounding after them. The shield

tumbled to the dusty ground. The wolf sniffed at it.

'Oi! Get away from that!' Lotta waved her arms.

Whetstone dusted himself down. 'So, we just have to get it back from the giant, terrifying, half-wolf, half-God, then Lotta keeps it. No more tricks?'

Hel nodded. 'Get the shield and it's yours. It's that easy.'

'Which means it isn't easy at all.'

Hel gave another skeleton grin, the skin around her eyes crinkling with glee.

Chapter Fourteen

Good Doggy

Two!

Four!

Six!

Eight!

Who do we appreciate?

TEEEEEAAAAM LOKI!

The Hel's Belles piled on top of each other, forming a human pyramid. Hel stuck a foot into the heap of cheerleaders and was boosted to the top. 'Get on with it,' she snapped at Whetstone and Lotta. 'I want to see Fenrir eat you.'

In the middle of the dusty field, Lotta jutted out her chin. 'Then you won't get the riddle.'

Hel grinned. 'Fenrir! Guard the shield!'

Fenrir curled his lip, a low growl rumbling out. The shield looked no bigger than a dinner plate compared to the monstrous wolf.

Lotta pulled the long sword out of the scabbard on her back. Whetstone shook his head. 'Why bother – unless you're planning on giving it to him as a toothpick?'

'It makes me feel better, OK? It's a comfort thing.'

The sword's point wobbled in the air. Whetstone eyed it. 'Are you sure you're all right?'

Lotta tossed her head and nearly overbalanced. 'Let's just get on with it.'

The giant wolf splayed out his front paws, lowering his head to the ground. 'Vali said he was a puppy – maybe he wants to play?' Whetstone muttered.

'Good. He can play *give me back my shield*,' Lotta replied through gritted teeth.

Whetstone stuck his shaking hands in his pockets, trying to block out the enormous wolf and calm his heartbeat. He ran his fingers over the leather pouch Hod had given him. He was sure the necklace was important somehow. If he could just figure it out. Maybe there was something special about the beads or the charms?

Lotta stepped in front of Whetstone. 'Are you listening? I need you to concentrate. You lead Fenrir away from the shield while I get it.'

'How?' Whetstone turned the pouch over in his pocket.

'I don't know! Be your normal annoying self. Maybe he'll want to eat you?'

Whetstone looked up. 'Why me? Why don't *you* get eaten?'

'Because I'm getting the shield.' Lotta gave an exasperated sigh. 'Fine, whatever. As long as one of us gets the shield. You go left, and I'll go right. He can't watch us both at the same time.' Lotta paused and then awkwardly touched him on the shoulder. 'We can do this. Let's go!' She stumbled away, tracing a large circle round the wolf. 'And don't forget – get the shield!'

'Yeah, yeah.'

Whetstone walked forward, wracking his brains for anything the Angry Bogey had taught him that might help. He didn't fancy giving Fenrir a smack on the nose and would probably need special equipment to grab him by the scruff of the neck.

The beast shifted, moving from side to side with little jumps. Whetstone approached with careful steps. On the edge of his hearing came the music again. Whetstone pushed it out of his mind; the last thing he needed was to be distracted by spooky tunes right now.

Despite her uneven footsteps, Lotta was quicker and was now level with Fenrir's front paws. Whetstone dragged his feet across the dusty ground. He really, *really* did not want to get any closer to Fenrir. He had left the Angry Bogey to get away from wolves, not to spend more time with them.

Fenrir woofed with a voice like one hundred dogs all barking at once, his head twisting from side to side as he tried to keep both children in view.

Lotta waved her sword and shouted. The wolf snapped his jaws, narrowly missing Lotta's heels as she dived out of the way.

'HEY!' Whetstone cried with a jolt. He ran forward, trying to attract the beast's attention. The wolf turned, and flying drool splattered all around the boy, covering the ground with puddles.

On the other side of Fenrir, Lotta leaned on the sword to lever herself up, her chest heaving. Whetstone shouted again, hoping to keep the wolf focused on him. Fenrir crept forward, his eyes fixed on Whetstone, his hackles rising. A low growl rumbled out, masking the strange music.

'SIT!' Whetstone yelled, doing his best impression of his

foster mother. The wolf cocked his head. 'Lie down! Good boy!'

Fenrir's ears twitched. Slowly, he stretched out his front paws and lowered his body to the ground. He sniffed at the boy. Whetstone tried to make himself smell inedible. The wolf wagged his tail. With amazement, Whetstone realized that Fenrir really *was* just a puppy. He wondered how big Fenrir would get when he was fully grown.

'Do you know any tricks?' Whetstone called, trying not to look at the enormous teeth. 'How about *roll over*?' Fenrir snapped at him playfully. 'Or *beg*?' Whetstone backed away, the wolf stretching his long body across the ground to follow him.

Something furry rubbed up against Whetstone's leg. The boy nearly jumped out of his skin. 'Mr Tiddles!' Whetstone tried to nudge the cat away with his foot. 'Get out of here, you stupid cat – you're going to get eaten!'

'He's not the only one,' said a man's voice.

Taking his eyes off the wolf for a moment, Whetstone spun round to see a stocky figure in a faded cloak. 'Hod?'

A grey-faced Vali stepped out from behind Hod, looking even more sour than usual. Whetstone hesitated as he took in the details of what he was seeing. Hod's hands were bound together with a stout rope.

'What's going on?'

'Whetstone, you need to get out of here,' Hod began. 'If your mother could see you playing with giant wolves, she would have a fit!'

Vali gave Hod a powerful shove. Music reverberated again.

Whetstone dodged sideways as Fenrir stretched out a huge paw. 'I'm not playing with it! We've got to get . . . Lotta's . . . shield.' The boy staggered round in a circle as his ears finally caught up with his brain. 'What do you mean *my mother*?'

The cat hissed, his fur rising. Fenrir panted, his breath wet and warm on the back of Whetstone's neck. Ignoring the wolf, Whetstone fixed his eyes on Hod and Vali as they approached Hel.

The Hel's Belles in the pyramid disassembled and re-formed as some kind of supernatural conveyor belt, passing Hel from hand to hand until she landed on the ground in front of Vali and Hod. A couple of the cheerleaders grabbed Hod's arms, and a third frisked him, turning out his pockets. Hod cringed away from their touch.

Hel's voice echoed across the dry field. 'Well, where is it?'

Vali crossed his arms. 'You don't even know what you're looking for.'

'I know that he has it, and that Daddy wants it.'

Just as Vali opened his mouth to retort, the music suddenly surged in volume. Piercing notes rang out, filling the huge field. The music fell into Whetstone's ears like drops of pure gold. Vali and Hel stared at each other dumbstruck. Fenrir paused in the act of closing his jaws around Whetstone's head.

'What was that?' Hel hissed.

Heart hammering, Whetstone ducked away from the slobbering wolf. He shoved his hand into his pocket as the sound rang out again. The necklace in its leather pouch pulsated in his hand. Whetstone untied the leather cords holding the pouch closed and a bright light shone out. Carefully, he tipped the necklace into his palm, all thoughts of the shield, Lotta and the danger they were in, gone. Between the coloured beads and ornaments, the thread that held the necklace together was glowing.

Whetstone lifted it up. The note rang out again. The light coming from the string grew until it was so bright Whetstone had to look away. The note rang out again and again, high and insistent.

'It's the harp string,' Whetstone whispered, ignoring Fenrir's movements behind him. 'But that must mean . . .' He turned back to look at Hod, who gave him a sad-eyed smile. 'Dad?'

Hel strode forward. 'That! That's what I'm looking for.' She held out a skeleton hand. 'Give it to me.'

Whetstone's hand instinctively closed over the necklace. 'No!'

'No?' Hel's eyes narrowed. 'I guess I'll just have to take

it, then.' Hel gestured towards Whetstone and the troupe of cheerleaders started to march towards him, their fingers flexing.

Whetstone backed away, the cat yowling as he was nearly stepped on. A shout came from behind. Wide-eyed, Whetstone spun round to face Fenrir, who was now staring at something near his tail. The wolf growled, the sound mixing with the persistent melody from the harp string.

Whetstone's stomach dropped. *Lotta.* Too late, he leaped forward, waving his arms to try to attract Fenrir's attention. The wolf ignored him, snapping down at something by his back leg.

In a flash of armour, Lotta was flung across the field. She landed with a crunch beside the Helhest cheerleaders. With a bark, Fenrir leaped after the fallen Valkyrie, knocking Whetstone on to the dusty ground.

'No!' Whetstone set off at a run, leaving the cat behind. His breath came in painful gasps, fear beating in his chest. If anything had happened to Lotta, it would be all his fault. He'd got distracted. He'd left her to get the shield by herself. Whetstone sprinted forward as Vali knelt beside Lotta. She didn't move.

Fenrir landed in front of Lotta and Vali. But to Whetstone's surprise, instead of swallowing them both in one enormous bite, the wolf wagged his tail and rolled over, showing his shaggy belly to the sky. Vali emerged from Fenrir's fur, giving Fenrir the world's biggest tummy rub. The wolf's back leg thrashed energetically, sending Hel's troupe of cheerleaders flying.

'Good boy, Fenrir,' Vali was saying as Whetstone skidded to a halt beside Lotta. 'You're a good boy.'

Whetstone dropped to his knees. A heavy weight settled in his stomach. The music faded, but the harp string still sparkled.

Lotta's eyes snapped open. Whetstone's heart lifted.

'Did you get it?' she murmured woozily.

'Get . . . it?' Whetstone's heart dropped back down like a stone.

Lotta pushed herself into a sitting position as Fenrir wiggled on his back, sending up clouds of dust. 'My shield, dummy! Where is it?'

Hel emerged through the dust storm. She placed one boot on Lotta's breastplate and shoved the Valkyrie back into the dirt. Lotta pushed ineffectively at Hel's foot. 'Get off me!'

Hel ignored her. Instead she focused on Whetstone, who gazed up at her, the scent of decay filling his nose.

'Do you want to tell her or shall I?'

'Pass me my shield.' Lotta's fumbling fingers reached for Whetstone. 'You're going to regret standing on me when I get my powers back, Hel!'

Hel gave a raspy giggle. Fenrir rolled over and sat up, shaking dust out of his shaggy coat.

Lotta's brown eyes followed as two of the Hel's Belles backflipped across the field to where the wolf had been sitting. The shield lay abandoned on the ground. 'No!' Lotta clawed at Hel's leg.

Whetstone scrambled to his feet. 'Give it back to her!'

'The shield is mine. I won it fair and square.' Hel snorted. 'Now give me the glowing string.'

'What is she talking about?' Lotta panted.

Whetstone showed her his hand. The harp string thrummed, glowing gently.

Lotta goggled. 'The necklace is the harp string?'

Hel reached out to wrench the string from Whetstone's hand. The boy lunged out of the way. He snatched up Lotta's sword, which was lying abandoned at her side, and got to his feet. Wrapping the string around the rusty blade, he threatened, 'I'll cut it – it'll be useless then!'

Hel stopped; her eyes narrowed. 'Cut the string and I'll do the same to your father.' The Hel's Belles tightened their grip on Hod.

Whetstone's eyes flicked from the glowing harp string to the man standing behind Hel. If Hel got her hands on the harp string, she would pass it to Loki in a heartbeat. But . . . Hod was his dad. He'd waited his whole life for this moment! For the chance to find his parents and have a family. Sweat prickled across his back. Could he really give up the opportunity to get to know his father, even to keep the harp string from Loki? The sword shook in his hand.

'Being a Hero is all about tough choices,' Hel continued. 'So I'll make it easier for you.' She pressed down on Lotta's breastplate, making the Valkyrie gasp. 'I'll throw the girl in for free. There's not much power left in her, anyway. She'll be a useless human by tomorrow.'

Whetstone tightened his grip on the sword, the string glowing against the dull blade.

'Is that string really worth more than your father and your friend?' Lotta thrashed on the ground, sending up more dust.

'Don't do it,' Hod called out. 'It's got strange magic—' One of the Hel's Belles clamped her hand over his mouth.

'You might as well get something out of this mess, Whetstone. I'm going to take the string one way or another,' Hel purred.

Whetstone bowed his head, his shoulders slumping. The harp string? Or Lotta and his dad? Surely Lotta was better off an alive human than a dead Valkyrie? She would understand. Hesitantly he lowered the sword and held out the necklace.

Hel snatched it out of his hand, triumph gleaming in her eyes. 'YES!' She removed her boot from Lotta's chest.

The Valkyrie rolled on to her hands and knees. 'What are you doing?' she wheezed. 'Have you gone mad?'

The Hel's Belles released Hod. They cheered and

whooped, shaking their pom-poms.

'You had to mess it up for all of us, didn't you?' Vali glared at Whetstone. 'You wanted to know why I came here? Father *never* visits Helheim – I should've been safe.' With shaking hands, Vali brushed the dust and dog hair from his clothes. 'But, thanks to you, he's coming.' Without another word, the stone boy turned and started the long walk back to the hall, followed by Fenrir.

'I'm looking forward to hearing the full riddle, Lotta. Although –' Hel waved the harp string – 'I've figured out the most important bits already.'

Lotta's fingers clenched into fists.

Hel fixed her eyes on the boy. 'I'm a better Hero than you,

Whetstone. You didn't get the shield, and you missed that my bridge keeper was your long-lost father.' Hel formed her hands into *L*s. 'You're no match for Team Loki.'

Whetstone ground his teeth.

The Helhest formed into a crooked horse and boosted Hel into the saddle. 'I can't wait to let Daddy know what I've done. He'll be so proud of me,' Hel preened. 'I'm sure he'll come straight here to see for himself.'

Whetstone swallowed the sour taste in his mouth.

'You've *lost*. Come back to my hall when you're ready. It's not as if it's possible to escape Helheim.' Laughing, Hel headed back to the Great Hall, the Helhest carrying the shield triumphantly after her.

Lotta glared at Whetstone. A Category Three Valkyrie Death Stare. Whetstone took a step back. Her eyes were tiny slits in her face. '*What. Did. You. Think. You. Were. Doing?*' she hissed.

'Well, I—'

'You. *Didn't*. Stick. To. The. Plan.'

'No, I—'

'The *only* thing I asked of you.' She poked him in the chest.

'I'm sorry. I was distracted—'

'You were supposed to be *distracting* Fenrir!'

'It was the necklace,' Whetstone explained. 'Hod—'

'Oh yes – I saw you had enough time for a little chat with him.' Lotta pointed a wavering finger at Hod.

'Come on,' Hod began. 'That's not fair.'

Lotta's glare ramped up to a Category Four. 'Now look

176

what you've done! Loki is coming, Hel still has my shield, you *gave* her the harp string and I'm trapped in Helheim with almost no powers and no way HOME!'

Whetstone glared back at her. 'This is not all about you! Will you stop going on about your stupid shield? It's *not* my fault you lost it. And your *brilliant plan* was rubbish! That's why it failed!'

'I think we should all calm down—' Hod began.

'Have you forgotten you *offered* Hel the riddle?' Whetstone continued, jabbing a finger at Lotta. 'You just *told* her you knew it! If Loki gets hold of the harp strings, there won't be an Asgard to go back to! Or a Midgard, or a Helheim. Hel will be able to go wherever she likes and bring all her monsters with her!'

'I told you I had that sorted,' Lotta sniffed. 'I just needed my shield, then I could've transformed and got us all out of here and got Scold to come back. But no – you had to muck it all up because you couldn't concentrate!'

'I thought you were DEAD!' Whetstone spluttered. 'Fenrir threw you across the field!'

'I'm a VALKYRIE! Well . . . I was. If I had all my powers, I would have hardly felt that.' The cat wound itself around her ankles. Lotta wobbled again. Whetstone reached out to take her arm. 'Don't touch me,' she snapped, twisting away. The cat gave Whetstone a very judgemental look. 'Odin was wrong about you – you're not a Hero. A Hero wouldn't be so SELFISH! Achoo!'

'Don't pretend you care about the quest and the harp

strings,' Whetstone snapped back. 'Ever since Freyja told you that your shield was in Helheim, that's all you've been thinking about.'

'At least I *tried* to help you. I saved you from Loki. I got you to Helheim—'

'You were more worried about that stupid cat! You say I'm selfish, but the only reason you've ever helped me is because you're worried about getting kicked out of Asgard for being a terrible Valkyrie!'

'I may not be the best Valkyrie, but I'm a better Hero than you'll ever be.' Lotta snatched the cat to her chest and turned on her heel.

'Fine, go! I don't need you!' Whetstone's hands balled into fists.

'I don't need you either.'

'Good!'

'Good!' Lotta stuck her drippy nose into the air and stomped away.

Whetstone watched her vanish into the settling dust. 'She chose to come back and help me,' he muttered, painfully aware that his father had heard everything. 'I never asked her to come.' *But you wanted her to*, a little voice in his head reminded him.

Chapter Fifteen

Unhappy Families

Whetstone and Hod stood alone in the dusty field. 'I'm sorry I didn't tell you before. Back at the bridge,' Hod began. 'I realized who you were when that girl said your name.' His beard twitched into a smile. 'Is she really a Valkyrie?'

Whetstone nodded and crossed his arms. He didn't want to think about Lotta. Hot and uncomfortable emotions bubbled inside him. It wasn't his fault Lotta hadn't got her shield. He *had* distracted Fenrir like she'd told him to. *She* should've tried harder.

'I never thought I would see you again.' Hod put his hand on Whetstone's shoulder, jolting him back into the present. 'The last glimpse I had of you was at the house by the lake.'

Whetstone's chest throbbed. Anger and embarrassment transforming into a hard lump of sorrow.

Hod peered into Whetstone's face. 'How is your mother?'

The lump swelled up to fill Whetstone's chest and made it hard to speak. He stared down at his boots.

Hod squeezed his shoulder. 'The strings took her too?'

Whetstone nodded.

'What about you?'

Whetstone forced back memories of his life with the Angry Bogey and her foster home for abandoned wolf cubs. Loki had taken him there after his parents disappeared so she could keep an eye on him. The Angry Bogey had always told Whetstone that he couldn't miss what he'd never had, but he did. He missed every day that had been stolen from him with his family. 'I stayed.'

Hod nodded. 'How long—?'

'Twelve years.'

'That's a long time.'

Whetstone swallowed with difficulty. 'What was it like,' he asked, not looking up. 'When we were all together?'

Hod's beard twitched into a smile. 'The house always used to smell of pinecones. Your mother used to save them up. On bad days she would put them on the fire. She liked that.'

Whetstone nodded, his vision blurring. He blinked his tears away.

'There are no pinecones here,' Hod murmured. 'And lots of bad days. Sometimes I wondered if I'd made the whole thing up.' He looked at Whetstone. 'But we're together again now. Come back with me to the bridge. It's not so bad there. You can smell the spring sometimes.' He grinned. 'Hey – when spring comes, I get so excited that I wet my plants, but at least I don't *soil* them!'

Whetstone lifted his head. 'Wait, you want us to stay here?'

Hod shrugged. 'Hel's right. No one leaves the Land of Lost Things.'

The lump of sorrow in Whetstone's chest cracked. Anger and disappointment poured through him until he felt as if he might burst. 'This can't be it! Everything I've done, everything I'm supposed to do . . . just to be stuck here forever.' He glared at his father, his face screwing up. 'You're my dad – you're supposed to make things better. Have you ever even *tried* to escape?'

'Of course I have,' the man snapped. 'But sometimes you have to accept the fact that you cannot change things, no matter how much you want to. I'm not a Hero, or a God. I was a fisherman. If you want someone to bait a line, I'm your man. If you want someone to rescue you from the Land of Lost Things, I can't help you.'

Hod took a deep breath, then spoke in a quieter voice. 'Do you know how many times I've wished I could change things? Go back and not pull those strings out of my fishing net?' He let out a hollow laugh. 'I thought I was so lucky to find them. We didn't have much, you know.'

Whetstone's anger began to drain away, leaving him cold and hollow inside. He closed his eyes, remembering the vision Loki had shown him of how his father had found the strings.

'There were three strings,' Hod continued softly. 'Caught round a falcon in my fishing net. How it got there I'll never know, a bird like that.'

Whetstone swallowed.

'I knew the strings were special. As fine as anything I had ever seen. Not even the local Chief's wife had anything like it.' Hod smiled at the memory. 'Your mother was so pleased when I showed them to her. We would have traded them eventually, but we decided that for that one night we were going to have one each and imagine ourselves fine lords and ladies. I gave one to you –' he nodded at Whetstone – 'one to your mother and kept the third for myself.'

Whetstone squeezed his hands into fists.

'But then they started to glow, like that one did back there with Fenrir. And all I could see was the light, and I felt like I was falling.'

Whetstone opened his eyes.

Hod shrugged. 'I woke up here in the snow, and I've been here ever since.'

'Loki was the falcon,' Whetstone said around the lump in his throat.

'Loki?'

Whetstone nodded. 'He stole a magic harp from the Dwarves. Those are the harp strings. The Dwarves cursed the strings to stop Loki using them by sending them into separate worlds . . . Because we were holding them, we were cursed too.' Whetstone rubbed his cheek. 'I don't know what happened to my harp string. I guess Loki must've hidden it somewhere. Now he's using me to find the other two.'

'And Odin wants you to stop Loki?' Hod said in amazement. 'The Valkyrie said that you were a Hero. My son, a Hero!' He grinned. 'Hey, if you can be a Hero, maybe there's some hope for me.'

Whetstone shoved his hands in his pockets, embarrassment washing over him. Lotta was right: some Hero he was turning out to be.

'You know, I never used to really believe all those stories about the Gods,' Hod said, stroking his beard. 'Before I came here, of course. It's a bit hard not to believe in Hel once you've met her. Something about her lingers.' Hod waggled his eyebrows.

'Yeah, the smell,' Whetstone muttered, smiling against his will. 'But why did the string glow just now? The Dwarves made the strings to let them cross between worlds, but no one was going anywhere.'

'It glows like that when danger is near,' Hod explained. 'You were about to be eaten. If your friend hadn't stomped on Fenrir's tail, you would have been a goner.'

'Lotta – her name is Lotta.' A hot rush of shame washed over him. 'I didn't know she did that.'

Hod was lost in thought for a moment. 'If you know where the strings are, does that mean you know where your mother is?'

'Sort of. There's a riddle, but it's not all that clear.' Whetstone hunched his shoulders. 'It doesn't matter anyway. I've failed. I gave Hel the harp string. Loki will come to collect it, and Lotta promised Hel the rest of the riddle.' Anger stabbed through him. 'Now there's nothing to stop Loki repairing the harp, then he'll be able to open the barriers between the worlds and fill them with monsters.'

'If there is one thing that living here has taught me,' Hod began, wrapping his arm round Whetstone's shoulders, 'it's that too many people arrive regretting the things they *didn't* do. It's not over – not yet – and you'll always regret it if you don't try to fix things with your friend and do everything you can to stop Loki.'

Whetstone bit his tongue. Lotta's face flashed into his mind. Guilt churned in his stomach.

'We're all allowed to make mistakes,' Hod continued. 'We just have to try and fix them too.'

❋

Reluctantly, Whetstone and Hod made their way back to the Great Hall. The sunken door swung open as they approached, candlelight flickering from inside while grating music filled the air.

'You know,' Hod said, stroking his beard, 'I've never actually been in there.'

'What, never?' Whetstone looked up in surprise. 'You never left the bridge?'

'Hel gave me a job to do.' Hod tapped the glasses in his pocket. 'I see them as they come in. That's enough for me.'

Whetstone wondered what he would see if he looked through the glasses, then he decided he was better off not knowing.

'Hey –' Hod nudged Whetstone with this elbow – 'guess who I bumped into on the way to get my glasses fixed? Everybody!'

Whetstone scuffed his toe through the footprints in the dust from the unwinnable race. 'Let's go inside. It can't be any worse than out here.'

'Are you sure?' Hod asked as they dipped inside.

Whetstone was wrong – it *was* worse. Helhest figures whirled around the room in a sort of dance, Fenrir snapping at them as they spun past his dog basket, while a Helhest orchestra played discordant music on a collection of lost instruments. Hod stopped on the stairs and gave a low whistle, taking it all in.

'It's a – a feast?'

A couple of the dancers whirled behind them, and blue-black strands of Helhest oozed across the doorway, trapping them inside.

Whetstone moved deeper into the room. 'I guess so.'

Sitting on a bench off to one side was Lotta. She very pointedly turned her back as Whetstone descended the steps. Vali sat opposite her, watching him over Lotta's shoulder. Their table was littered with bowls and plates of rotting food. Whetstone held his sleeve over his mouth and tried not to breathe in the sickly scent.

At the far end of the hall, Hel sat on her spindly throne, a goblet in her skeletal hand and the harp-string necklace tied round her neck. She stood up. 'Whetstone, you're late to the party! I've invited Daddy – he should be here soon!' The light shimmered, momentarily revealing ghostly forms filling the hall.

'Her powers are getting stronger,' Hod muttered.

Hel took a swig from her goblet. 'It's time for the poetry – Lotta is just about to give me the riddle.'

Lotta made a noise halfway between a laugh and a sob.

185

Her circular shield was back on the wall behind Hel, one of the sections flickering on and off. It's not too late, Whetstone realized. Lotta still had *some* powers left.

'Why don't you start us off?' Hel hiccupped. 'Vali said you were good at poems!'

Whetstone glanced at Vali, who picked at his nails with his knife.

'Come on!' Hel encouraged. 'I'll even give you the first line.' She threw out her human arm and recited:

A boy once came to Helheim,
And he thought that everything was fine . . .

She nodded at Whetstone. 'Go on.'

Whetstone thought for a moment.

He wants to go home,
So throw him a bone,
And let us all out this time?

Hel cackled, throwing herself back in her seat. 'Good one! How about this.' She continued:

You came to the Land of the Dead,
But you're in far over your head.
You want to go free,
But all belongs to me.
You'll just have to stay here instead!

The ghostly forms flickered as Hel giggled.

Whetstone screwed up his face. 'I've seen better feasts.' He peered around the room. 'Where's all the eating and axe throwing? You know, the *actual* feasting?'

'Oh, I'm sure we could arrange for someone to throw axes at you, if that's what you want,' Vali offered. Whetstone ducked as a knife spun across the room. Lotta hunched her shoulders.

'Careful, we need him alive. For now.' Hel took another swig from the goblet, a dark liquid draining between her pointed teeth. Round her neck, the harp string glittered.

Whetstone slumped on a bench next to his father. No one ever wanted him alive for something nice.

On the other side of the room, Lotta dragged her fingers across the table, leaving greasy streaks in the polish. Her head felt heavy, her thoughts slowing down. She doodled a picture of a Viking boy on the table. Lotta had been worried about Whetstone being stuck in Krud. She had thought they were friends. That's why she went to all the effort of borrowing Awfulrick's cup to make sure she won the poetry contest. What a waste of time that had been. A sour taste rose in her throat. In her drawing, she added arrows sticking out of the boy's head. She sniffed and rubbed her hands over the picture, wiping it out.

Vali leaned across the table. 'Do you know what I miss the most?'

Lotta shook her head. The cat wound around her legs, making her itch.

'The bronze sky. In Asgard the sky was always bronze. It took me ages to get used to a blue sky in Midgard, and here . . .' He shrugged.

'I miss the smell of Valhalla,' Lotta offered.

'What – big sweaty men, overcooked sausages and sharp weapons?'

Lotta nodded morosely. 'I never should have left. I was so pleased with myself when I won that contest. But it was all a trick to get rid of me.'

One of Hel's tattered birds flew the length of the hall and landed on the back of her throne. Lotta thought of Odin's ravens bringing him news from across the Nine Worlds. She scratched at the tabletop. Odin would be furious when he found out they had failed to get the harp string. If he ever came back from Jotunheim, that is. Tears burned in the corners of her eyes; she blinked them away. Valkyries didn't cry, and she was still a Valkyrie. Just.

Hel stepped down from her throne and swept past them, her eyes twinkling. Lotta's stomach flipped – there was only one thing that could make Hel look so pleased with herself. Loki must be on his way.

Vali watched his sister go. 'She writes to him. Father, I mean. That's how she told him you were here.'

Loki. The shapeshifter who was determined to hunt them down all because of a stupid riddle and some stupid harp strings. Lotta dug her nails into her palms. If only she'd never met Whetstone! She would be safe up in Asgard, probably polishing some armour or something. Glinting-Fire wouldn't be trying to get rid of her, and she'd be just another ordinary Class Three Valkyrie. Her vision blurred for a second. Behind Hel's throne the shield gave another flicker.

Vali was still talking. Now that he had started, the words just kept on coming. Lotta tried to focus on what he was saying. ' . . . she can't get over the fact that he abandoned her, and their mum is just as bad. I mean, you've met Jormungandr, Fenrir is OK, but—'

'Wait a minute.' Lotta tapped her fingers on the table. 'You said she writes to him. She has a way of sending letters to Asgard?'

Vali nodded. 'Not exactly letters. It used to drive my mum mad.'

❊

Whetstone slouched on his bench, trying not to watch Lotta and Vali chatting like old friends. Whetstone had thought that Lotta didn't like Vali. No one in Asgard seemed to like Vali. When Whetstone first met him, Vali was a weird, knife-obsessed loner and Whetstone didn't think he'd improved, even if he was a Troll now. Whetstone knew he should go over and apologize, but his feet didn't want to move. It was easier to stay sitting here, bad thoughts churning in his head.

Hod leaned forward, breaking into Whetstone's angry thoughts. 'Hel's gone.'

Whetstone's head snapped towards the white throne. It was empty.

'She left,' Hod explained. 'While you were busy sulking.'

'I was not sulking,' Whetstone spluttered.

On the other side of the hall, Vali said something to Lotta, who nodded. They both got to their feet and headed towards a narrow doorway almost hidden in the shadows.

'Now, where are they off to?' wondered Hod aloud.

❁

'In here.' Vali slipped through the doorway.

Lotta followed, catching her knee on a bench on the way. The world around her felt fuzzy. She was NOT turning human, she told herself. She was going to get her shield and get back to Asgard so she could kick Flee and Flay on the bottom. She just needed to FOCUS.

She paused on the threshold, taking in the horror that was Hel's bedroom. Lotta didn't know what she was expecting. A four-poster bed with curtains of darkest night and pillows stuffed with lost souls maybe? She definitely was not expecting the untidy piles of clothes, broken cuddly toys and abandoned goblets on every surface. A narrow bed with rumpled blankets was pushed up against one wall; the floor was littered with screwed-up drawings. 'And I thought my room was a mess.'

Lotta crept forward. A piece of paper caught around her boot. She peeled it off and uncrumpled it, revealing a black-and-white drawing. *Mume, Dady, Jorm, Fenrir and me* was written across the bottom in careful loopy writing. One of the figures was snake-like, the other a dog. Lotta dropped the paper again.

Vali stopped in front of a gooey black wall. 'Whatever you write on this wall will appear back in our house in Asgard. She used to write all the time. My mum hung a tapestry up in front of it in the end.'

Lotta's blood pounded in her ears. 'This is it! This is how we get home.'

Vali ran his hand over his hair. 'We can send a message, but there's no guarantee anyone will see it. Mum covered up the other wall, remember? I know Hel thinks Father is on his way, but he might not even have seen the message yet.'

Lotta stepped closer to examine the wall. 'What's it made of?'

'No idea.' Vali wrinkled his nose. 'I think Father made it on one of his good days.'

'What's going on?' said a voice from behind them.

Lotta and Vali spun around to see Whetstone standing in the doorway, his hands stuffed in his pockets. Lotta turned her back on him, wobbling as the room spun. 'Mind your own business.'

Whetstone stepped into the cluttered room. 'Look, Lotta,' he said, staring at the ground, 'I'm sorry about the shield thing. I was so worried about you being hurt that I forgot about getting it. I should've realized that you getting the shield back was just as important as . . . my stuff. I should've tried harder to help you.'

Lotta sniffed. Vali raised his eyebrows in a sceptical expression.

Whetstone looked up. 'Seriously. We've got a bit of time: the shield is still glowing. If we work together and convince Hel to give us another chance –' Whetstone stopped. 'What?'

Lotta turned back round, her brown eyes curiously wet. 'Whetstone, you are a complete pillock.' She marched across the room and thumped him on the arm.

Whetstone rubbed his bruise. 'I almost missed this.'

Vali crossed his arms. 'I wouldn't trust him if I were you. He's the one who got you into this mess.'

'Actually, that was the other Valkyries. I was an innocent bystander.' Whetstone grinned. Vali snorted.

'We've found a way of talking to Asgard.' Lotta gestured at the wall.

'But no-body-is-read-ing-it,' Vali reminded her.

Lotta tossed her head; the movement left her unbalanced. She touched the wall to steady herself, it sucked at her fingers. 'Vali, don't you think your mum will be looking for you?' She wiped her hand on her skirt and turned to Whetstone. 'Sigyn, his mum, kept badgering Odin to bring Vali back from Midgard. Once she even barged in when the Class Two Valkyries were showing Odin their flying formation. Scold was so cross I thought her head was going to explode.' Lotta faced Vali. 'And now you've completely vanished. Don't you think your mum would be so worried that she would even check the messages from Hel?'

Vali ran his hand through his dark hair and stuck out his jaw. 'Maybe.'

'But who in Asgard would help us?' Lotta mused. 'Sigyn wouldn't be able to get us out of Helheim – no offence.' Vali shrugged.

'And we need to get the harp string back too,' Whetstone added anxiously. 'Preferably before Loki gets it.'

The sound of Hod's raised voice rang out from across the Great Hall. '. . . fresh air. Too stuffy in here with all these candles . . .'

'Quick,' Whetstone hissed, pushing open the bedroom door. 'Dad was on lookout duty. Hel must be back. We have to get out of here.'

'Hey, Hel. Do you want to hear a joke?' Hod continued, a tinge of fear in his voice.

'Oh no, not the jokes,' Lotta moaned, scuttling outside, followed by Vali.

'How do you make a tissue dance? Put a little bogey in it!'

'We have to get Hel out of the hall,' Lotta muttered. 'That way we can – LEAVE ME ALONE, WHETSTONE!' she yelled as Hel suddenly turned towards them. Lotta winked at him. 'I'm not interested in anything you have to say!' She dropped back down on to the bench. Vali sat down opposite her, a knife twisting between his fingers. The cat blinked its yellow eyes at them and curled up on the end of the table.

'I'll do it,' Whetstone muttered as he faked sulking away. 'This sounds like a job for a Hero.'

Chapter Sixteen

Stuck in Helheim

Hel almost skipped across the Great Hall, the necklace gleaming in the candlelight. Behind her, Hod scratched his head.

'You're in a good mood.' Whetstone moved out of the way as Hel swirled through the Helhest dancers towards the throne.

'Yes –' she did a little spin, her cobweb hair flying out – 'and wouldn't you like to know why.' Whetstone tried not to choke as the smell of decay wafted towards him.

His eyes flickered over to Lotta and Vali. Vali stared down at his hands, his knuckles white. Lotta's jaw was clenched. Loki must be nearby. They had to get the shield and the harp string and get out.

Now.

Whetstone pushed his shoulders back. 'So, Hel, I've been thinking.'

'Have you?' Hel tucked her rotten legs up under her on the throne. 'Did it hurt?'

'It's just that the only reason I couldn't get the shield away from Fenrir was because Lotta was slowing me down.' From the corner of his eye he saw Fenrir prick up his ears. 'You saw how rubbish she was at the race. We only won because of my brilliant idea. I bet if I tried by myself, I could get the shield, no problem.'

The bench scraped as Hod scrambled across the room. He put his arm round Whetstone's shoulders. 'Ha ha, just a little joke. The boy's funny.' He tried to lead Whetstone away.

'It's not a joke.' Whetstone shrugged his father's arm away. 'Set up the challenge again, and I bet I can get it.'

'What are you doing?' Hod hissed, a fixed smile on his face. 'You only just escaped last time.'

Hel tapped her bony fingers against her jaw in thought.

'What have you got to lose? You've already got the harp string, and Lotta's promised you the riddle,' Whetstone continued. 'Why do you care if Fenrir eats me?'

Hel drummed her fingers against the arm of her throne.

'*You lot are all losers, you see,*
'*And that's all you will ever be.*
'*I'll give you a go,*
'*I won't be sorry, I know—*'

'*So how about two out of three?*' Whetstone finished, not looking at his father, who shook his head in despair.

'All right,' Hel said after a moment. She stood up. 'If you want to lose again, that's fine by me.'

'But just me this time. I don't need any help from this lot.'

Whetstone jerked a thumb at Lotta and Vali. Lotta snorted. 'Me against Team Loki.'

Hel tilted her head, the dark half of her hair covering her face. 'Oh yes. Team Loki.'

❄

Once again Whetstone found himself on the field, the Great Hall squatting low against the sky behind him, the wolf waiting in front. Lotta's shield lay gleaming in the red sunlight between Fenrir's enormous paws.

Hod stood off to one side, his arms crossed. Whetstone knew his father didn't understand why he was so determined to face the wolf, but he had to give Lotta and Vali a chance to contact Asgard. He was not staying here for the rest of his life – and death.

Whetstone clenched his hands into fists. His dad was right. He would regret it if he didn't try his hardest to stop Loki. And his mum was still out there somewhere. He couldn't just leave her. It wasn't as though Loki was going to stop chasing him.

Hel climbed back into her Helhest throne. It looked grander this time, with a canopy and footrest. She sipped a black drink with a black umbrella sticking out of it, a pair of dark glasses hiding her face. The necklace hummed gently against her neck, filling the still air with its music. The Hel's Belles lined up on either side of the throne. They looked less like cheerleaders now and more like soldiers. She was really

going all out to impress Loki, Whetstone thought, glancing up at the sky. He wondered how the Trickster would arrive. He was supposed to have a pair of Sky-walking Shoes. Maybe he would walk down?

'Same rules as before,' Hel barked. 'Get the shield away from Fenrir to win.'

Except he didn't have to win; he just had to keep them busy. Whetstone wiped his sweaty hands on his trousers, hoping that whoever Lotta contacted in Asgard got here quickly. And was good with wolves.

Left in the Great Hall, Lotta turned to Vali. 'Let's go.'

Vali stabbed his knife point down into the table. 'It's not going to work.'

'It's the only chance we have.'

'Mum won't be able to do anything. She never leaves Asgard.'

Lotta smiled. 'We're not going to ask her – we're going to ask someone else.'

'Who?'

Lotta's boots echoed as she stumbled across the hall. With reluctance, Vali pushed himself to his feet and followed, his knife left point-down in the table.

Stepping back into Hel's bedroom, Lotta shuffled carefully through the mess to reach the sticky black wall. 'How does it work?'

Vali loomed over her shoulder – for someone made of stone, he could move surprisingly quietly. 'I think whatever you write on the wall just appears on our wall in Asgard.'

'You *think*?'

Vali shrugged. 'I've never tried it.' He handed Lotta a small pot of white paint. 'There's not much left.'

'I'd better not write much then.' The brush came out of the paint pot with a sucking noise. Strings of slime clung to it. Lotta frowned, trying not to get it on her trembling fingers.

The Valkyrie lifted the brush to the wall, her tongue sticking out of the corner of her mouth in concentration. A couple of busy minutes later the message read:

TELL FREYJA
WE HAVE MR TIDLES
STUCK IN HELHEIM
COME QUIK!

Vali looked at it appraisingly. 'Well done – you spelled "quick" wrong, and "Tiddles" has two *d*s, but other than that it's not bad. I'd give it a solid six out of ten.'

Lotta trod on his foot with her heavy boot. Vali sighed. 'I'm stone, remember?'

Lotta brushed an escaped curl out of her face, accidentally leaving a trail of white blobby paint across her coppery cheek. A gust of warm air blew her hair back again. 'Wow, Vali. What have you been eating? Your breath stinks.'

'That's not my breath.'

Lotta's fingers clenched on the paint pot. She pivoted slowly, trying not to move any more than necessary.

Sticking through the doorway behind them was half an enormous paw, long black claws poking out of pale grey fur. A wet black nose the size of a bucket forced its way in. The air filled with dog breath.

'You've grown again, Fenrir.' Vali pushed the wolf back through the doorway. 'Shouldn't you be outside?'

The wolf gave a yip, which rattled the rafters. His wagging tail sent a table flying across the Great Hall.

Lotta's palms turned sweaty against the paint pot. 'But if this is Fenrir, then where are Hel and Whetstone?'

201

Outside under the red sun, the wolf growled. Long and low like something you might hear before an earthquake. It rumbled across the ground, travelled through Whetstone's boots and vibrated up his spine. The rumbling was the reason his legs turned to jelly, not the terror, Whetstone told himself.

The boy walked towards the wolf mentally reciting, *Fenrir's just a puppy – a really, really, really massive puppy. He won't hurt me. He just wants to play.* Whetstone bent down to tug off a boot. He waved it in the air. 'Want to play fetch, boy?'

The wolf barked sharply. His movements were more controlled, less puppy-like than before, his enormous eyes focusing on the boy rather than the boot. The wolf prowled closer.

The harp music grew in volume, filling Whetstone's ears with a sound like honey. A creeping chill ran up his spine. *Danger!* Behind him, Hod cried out. Whetstone kept his eyes focused on the wolf's curved teeth. 'Not now, Dad.'

'Yes, now,' replied Hel.

Whetstone spun round to see Hel holding a knife to Hod's throat with one hand, twisting his arm up behind his back with the other. Hod gripped on to Hel's knife arm, his fingers slipping on the smooth bone.

'Let him go!' Whetstone shouted. 'This isn't part of the deal.'

'Eyes on the prize, Whetstone. No one cares about the silly shield.'

The harp string rang out again, glowing white against Hel's neck.

A blast of dog breath hit the boy from behind. Whetstone turned round slowly. Long white rocks and a dark, dripping cave filled his vision. It took a moment for him to realize he was staring into the wolf's open mouth. He flinched backwards, sprawling on the ground as Hel giggled.

❀

Lotta held her breath and squeezed past Fenrir, his thick fur blocking the way to the Great Hall. Fear churned in her stomach. Hel had tricked them. She had to find Whetstone – he'd be in deep trouble.

'Get off, Fenrir. Urgh, I'm covered in dribble now.' Vali had made it through to the Great Hall and, by the sounds of it, Fenrir was giving him a good wash.

Lotta pushed through the endless fur. She could stretch out her whole arm and still touch nothing but hair. 'At least it's not a cat,' she muttered as fur tickled her nose.

She popped out into the candlelight. Vali stood in a puddle of drool, his clothes damp and his face wet. He shoved his hair out of his face with one hand and held Fenrir off with the other. The wolf had indeed grown larger. He now filled the space inside the Great Hall, looming over the piles of Lost Things.

Lotta looked around apprehensively. Except for them, the hall was empty. 'Where are Hel and Whetstone?'

Vali wiped the drool off his face. 'Not here. I knew she agreed too easily.' He glanced around. 'Where's the cat? The last thing we need is for Freyja to turn up and find out we've lost it.'

A yowl answered him. Mr Tiddles was perched on the back of Hel's throne, his fur sticking straight up so he resembled a dandelion.

'I'll get the cat – you look for Hel.' Lotta tentatively placed a foot on the platform, wary in case she got stuck like she had when they first arrived. But the power must lie with Hel, and as she was not in the room Lotta climbed on to the platform easily, even though her knees wobbled from the effort.

Lotta gazed longingly at the empty space on the wall behind the throne where her shield had been displayed, before tearing her eyes away.

'Come on, Mr Tiddles. Achoo!' Lotta started prising the cat off the chair, the cat's claws scoring long scratches into the frame.

Fenrir wagged his tail, smashing benches and piles of Lost Things aside before lunging for Vali again. Lotta watched them from the platform. 'You know, of all your relatives, I think he's my favourite.'

Vali climbed out from under his younger brother's paws. 'Let's get out of here.'

'Achoo!' Lotta clutched the cat to her chest and scrambled down to make her way to the stairs. She stopped. 'The door has gone.'

Vali peered over Fenrir's shoulder. 'What do you mean? It's a door – it can't be gone.'

Lotta staggered up the worn steps, which now led up to a blank stretch of wall, her breath coming in gasps. She ran her hand over the space, hoping the door was still there and that her eyes were playing tricks on her. Her fingertips found solid wood and clay. Lotta's heart sped up; her skin prickled. 'She's trapped us.' She turned to Vali. 'Is there another way out?'

'I don't think so. That's the only door.'

Fenrir barked, making Lotta's head ring. His tail swiped back and forth, turning benches to toothpicks. A candlestick flew towards her, bouncing up the stairs before landing at Lotta's feet. An idea occurred to her as she bent to pick it up. 'We'll just have to make our own door, then. Fenrir, can you play fetch?'

The wolf snapped his jaws excitedly. Vali clambered out of the way as Fenrir tensed his shoulders, his eyes fixed on the shiny object.

'FETCH!' Lotta threw the candlestick as high and as far

across the room as she could. The enormous wolf jumped
after it. He overshot, his back slamming into the corner where
the wall met the ceiling. With a splintering crash, the wolf
vanished, leaving a jagged hole behind him.

Lotta choked, the air full of dust and splinters, the cat
squirming in her arms. She wiped her nose on her shoulder.
'Achoo! Achoo!'

Just visible through the dust, a pair of pointed furry ears
poked up from the other side of the hole.

'OK, that's one way to get out,' Vali conceded, dusting
himself off.

Dark shadows rushed towards the wall, stretching to

fill the gap with gooey tar-like strands.

'More Helhest!' Lotta scrabbled towards the broken wall, dust catching in her chest. 'How much of that stuff is there?'

Vali and the trainee Valkyrie scrambled up piles of broken benches to reach the hole in the wall. 'Achoo! I really don't want to be here when Hel finds out what we've done to her hall. Achoo!'

'Agreed.' Vali nodded, jumping through the hole. Lotta followed. Outside, Fenrir barked and wagged his tail. He dropped something at their feet: a very dribbly candlestick.

'Good boy.' Vali reached up to scratch Fenrir behind the ears. The wolf closed his eyes and twitched his back leg.

Lotta rubbed her sore eyes and shook the rubble out of her armour. Behind Fenrir, a howl pierced the air.

They all froze.

Vali's skin turned a pale grey, gleaming like flagstones in the rain. 'Oh no.'

Chapter Seventeen

A Cold Day in Hel

Whetstone sprawled backwards on the ground, desperate to avoid the wolf's gaping jaws. The wolf barked a laugh, then threw his head back in a howl. The sound cut across the landscape like a knife. Terrible, mournful and old. Hel giggled, holding her blade steady at Hod's throat.

The enormous wolf reared up on his back legs, his dark shape blotting out the sun. The howl changed tone, sharpening and breaking up into a man's laugh. Fear gripped Whetstone's insides with icy fingers as, with a whirl of grey fur, the wolf vanished. In his place was a tall, handsome man in a red tunic. The man shook his blond hair out of his face and smiled. 'Hello, Whetstone.'

Blood thudded loudly in Whetstone's ears. Dark spots danced in front of his eyes.

Loki.

Loki was here.

And there was no way out.

The boy dug his fingers into the hard ground, the soil building up beneath his fingernails, his mind desperate to block out the man in front of him.

Hod struggled against Hel's grip, but her thin fingers were surprisingly strong. She dragged him forward. Whetstone snatched his hand out of the way of their boots and scrambled to his feet, his heart pumping as if it was going to jump out of his chest.

'I told you he was here,' Hel simpered. 'Haven't I done well, Daddy?'

Loki smiled more broadly, the scars on his face pulling his lips into strange shapes. He brushed dust off his fine clothing. 'Indeed. Very clever.'

What was left of Hel's cheeks went pink. The harp string thrummed again. Whetstone coughed, trying to mask the sound.

'Thank you, Whetstone. I wouldn't have been able to do this without you.' Loki gestured at the string glowing round Hel's neck. 'I think that's mine.'

Whetstone watched horror-struck as Hel changed her grip to tug the necklace from her neck and toss it towards Loki.

With a sudden lunge, Whetstone launched himself upwards, snatching the bright string out of the air before it could reach the smiling man. He landed badly, stumbling and falling on to his side. Beads and charms flew everywhere, landing soundlessly on the dry ground. One made its way into Whetstone's boot. The string blazed white, dazzling Whetstone's eyes. It was like holding a sunbeam in his hands.

Loki walked forward, his soft boots leaving no marks in the earth. He stood over the boy. 'Give it to me.'

Whetstone took a deep breath. This time he was going to face Loki down properly and be the Hero. Lotta wasn't here to help him; he would have to do this alone. Whetstone stood up slowly, pain shooting up his leg. 'No.' His palms were sweaty; he doubled his grip, worried that the string might slip out of his grasp. 'This belongs to the Dwarves.'

'Why give it back to them? They wouldn't use its full powers.' Loki looked into Whetstone's eyes. 'Wouldn't you like to see what the Skera Harp can do?'

Whetstone felt a tickle in his mind. More power than he could ever have imagined, right at his fingertips . . . The Dwarves had designed the harp as a way of travelling between the Nine Worlds, to impress the Gods and display their skills. Whetstone's mind was filled with all the things he could do and all the places he could see if he had the Skera Harp. He could walk into Asgard whenever he liked. He could visit the Elves or the Fire Giants, find treasures, explore new lands . . . That would prove to everyone that he was special, not just a scruffy nobody from nowhere.

But Whetstone knew it wouldn't be like that. The Dwarves had destroyed the harp to prevent Loki from getting his hands on it. Loki wanted to use the harp's powers, not to travel between worlds, but to break down the walls that separated them. Without the walls there would be nothing to stop all the Giants and monsters destroying everything in their path. A vision of Hel marching into Krud flashed through his mind. Loki would use the chaos to his own advantage and people would get hurt. People had already been hurt. Whetstone shook his head.

'No? Pity. I thought you had more ambition.' Loki gestured towards Hod. 'But then look at your useless family. It's no wonder you're so spineless.'

Before Whetstone could protest, crackling green ropes wrapped round his father, lifting him into the air. Hel giggled, jumping out of the way. She clapped her hands.

'What are you doing to him? Stop!' Whetstone squeezed the harp string as it tingled against his palm.

'Why do you always have to make everything so difficult?' Loki mused, walking forward as Whetstone backed away. Hod rose higher. 'We could be friends, Whetstone. But helping your friends isn't something you're very good at, is it?'

Whetstone flushed. 'You're not my friend, Loki.'

Loki sighed. The ropes of green light surrounding Hod contracted. The man gave a muffled grunt.

'But I could be. I'm being more than generous,' Loki continued. 'Give me the harp string and I promise to return you, and that –' he jerked a thumb towards Hod, who had gone a very peculiar colour – 'to Midgard. Alive. And in one piece. Give me the rest of the riddle and I'll even help you rescue your mother.'

'Whetstone, don't—' Hod managed to gasp before the ropes wrapped round his mouth.

'What about Lotta?'

'What about her?' Loki sighed and straightened his cuffs. 'Your *friend* can stay here with Hel.' He grinned at his daughter. 'She'll be some company for you.'

'What – like Vali is?' Whetstone said. 'He's here too.'

'So?'

'So, you're just going to abandon them all?'

'I'm not abandoning anybody. When I open the walls, they can walk home.' Loki smiled. 'Not that there will be much of Asgard left after I let the Frost Giants in. Then, without me to do their thinking for them, everyone will see how pathetic Odin and the other Gods really are.'

'You're destroying the Nine Worlds because you're *jealous* of Odin?' Whetstone said in astonishment.

Footsteps thudded behind him. Lotta skidded to a stop, throwing up a shower of dust. 'That's not Fenrir!' The fluffy cat leaped out of her arms. 'Achoo!'

'Yeah, I noticed,' Whetstone muttered, his eyes fixed on Loki.

Lotta rubbed her red eyes and peered at the Trickster. 'Oh.'

A blast of dog breath hit them. Vali and the real Fenrir

stopped a short distance away. Vali ran his hand through his hair and leaned against the wolf's shoulder.

'Odin has had his chance,' Loki continued. 'It is time for the Nine Worlds to be reordered.'

'With you in charge, I suppose?' Lotta spluttered.

'Why not?' Loki smiled. 'All things must change. Even the Valkyries know that, now that Glinting-Fire is their leader.'

'And have you told this Glinting-Fire about your fabulous plan?' Whetstone huffed. 'Isn't the whole point of the Valkyries to bring Heroes to Valhalla? If anyone can go wherever they like, they're out of a job.'

'The Valkyries will adapt. Glinting-Fire has a new plan for the humans of Midgard.'

'Like what?' Lotta demanded.

Loki waved a hand dismissively. 'I don't know all the details. Something about Hero training camps. Put the humans through regimented training to weed out the weaklings.' His white teeth glinted as he smiled. 'She believes it will be more efficient than waiting for humans to prove themselves in battle, and Glinting-Fire loves efficiency.'

'That's terrible!' Whetstone gasped.

A hiss escaped between Lotta's teeth.

'Freyja was right.' Whetstone took a step. 'Glinting-Fire got rid of Lotta to stop her warning us. And you sent Odin away so there was no one to stop Glinting-Fire!'

Loki narrowed his eyes. 'Why should our lives be dictated by Odin and his cronies? They're bullies, Whetstone. Even to the other Gods. They went to war with the Vanir and forced

213

them into Vanaheim. Trapped the Fire Giants in Muspell and banished poor Hel to the Land of the Dead.' Hel gave a simpering smile.

'They had to do those things,' Lotta protested, 'to protect the Nine Worlds. And, anyway, it's not that simple. You're a Fire Giant and you're not in Muspell.'

'I never did understand why the Gods let you live with them in Asgard,' Whetstone muttered.

'Even the Gods know their limitations,' Loki purred. 'They need me, and Odin knows it.' He focused on Whetstone. 'The Gods are no better than you or me. They don't care about you humans in Midgard – they're too wrapped up in their own lives. If Odin is so powerful, where is he now, in your hour of need? Off having adventures of his own. I say it is time for change. Let the strongest, the cleverest, the bravest rise to the top and the so-called *Gods* can find their place just like the rest of us.'

Whetstone took a step backwards. 'But if you start mixing the worlds together, it will be chaos! The Nine Worlds will fall and it will be the end of everything!'

'I always thought there was something beautiful about chaos,' Hel mused. 'If you smash a mirror, you get the prettiest rainbows.'

'And someone usually gets cut,' Lotta muttered.

Hel's skeleton grin widened.

'You fought to change your fate, Whetstone,' Loki said, almost kindly. 'You were nothing. Now look at you.'

'That was different!'

214

'Was it? You wanted to be greater than you were: a poor orphan with nothing to call his own except his fleas. I'm planning the same thing, just on a larger scale.'

Whetstone and Lotta looked at each other. Lotta's shield gleamed, forgotten in the dust.

Loki held out his hand. 'Give me the harp string. I'm offering you everything you ever wanted. You can be with your parents again on Midgard. One big happy family.'

'Until the Giants and the dragons arrive. Or Glinting-Fire forces us into training camps.' Whetstone fought down a laugh. 'And what would you know about happy families anyway, Loki?'

Hel's eyes narrowed. 'We can be happy now. Can't we, Daddy? Fenrir is here – we just need Jorm and Mummy and we're all together again.'

Loki fixed his eyes on Whetstone. 'Enough talking. Give me the harp string willingly, or I'll take it from you.'

'Like you took my harp string, the one tied round my wrist when I was a baby? What did you do with it?'

The Trickster just smiled.

Whetstone fixed his eyes on Loki's handsome face. 'Odin sent me to stop you.' He stuffed the harp string into his pocket. 'Maybe you're right and the God's don't care about us, but *I* care, and *I'm* going to stop you.'

Loki's face curved into a snarl.

'It's all right, Daddy.' Hel laid her hand on her father's arm. 'Because that one –' she pointed at Lotta – 'has already promised me the riddle, and Valkyries always keep their promises. Isn't that right?'

Whetstone gulped – in the excitement he had forgotten about Lotta's promise to Hel.

Lotta grinned. 'Oh yes. The riddle.' A dry wind whipped through her hair, tugging at her curls. 'Are you sure you want it?'

Hel's needle teeth gleamed. 'Yes!'

'Lotta,' Whetstone began.

Loki narrowed his eyes.

'The riddle as told to me by the magic cup of Chief Awfulrick, which knows the fates of all men?' Lotta clarified, shuffling a few steps. 'I left it in Asgard, you know.'

'YES!' hissed Hel.

Whetstone's heart thumped loudly. She couldn't be about to tell everyone the location of his parents and the cursed harp strings, could she? Whetstone forced himself to relax. Lotta would have a plan. Probably.

Loki crossed his arms. Hel's fingers flexed as though she was going to snatch the riddle out of the air.

'He who can solve the riddle will learn the identity of something desired by humans and Gods alike!' Lotta announced. She threw open her arms and boomed at the top of her voice:

'I am round, but I am not a wheeeeeel.'

Whetstone tried to hide his bafflement. He had no idea what she was talking about.

'I am made of flour, but I do not grow.
I am hard, but I crumble in water.
You can hold me and my brothers in your hand.
What am I?'

Her voice died away. Whetstone stared at his feet, desperate not to laugh.

'That's the riddle?' Vali spluttered.

Lotta nodded. 'It's *a* riddle. As spoken by the magic cup. It's not my fault you didn't specify which riddle you were after.'

Vali leaned on Fenrir's shoulder, weak with laughter. 'Well done, sis. You got your riddle!'

Hel looked from Vali to Lotta, pink spots appearing on her lifeless cheeks. 'You're not a real Valkyrie,' she spat. 'You're a cheat!'

'I'm a different sort of Valkyrie,' Lotta retorted proudly. 'And you're a sore loser!'

'You'll regret upsetting my daughter.'

Loki opened his hand – a palmful of green sparks glinted there. The man threw them high into the air. Dark clouds rushed in from the horizon, blotting out the red sun.

The harp string thrummed again and Hod dropped to the ground with a thud. Whetstone managed one step towards him before a freezing cold wind pushed him back.

Lotta shivered and slumped against Whetstone's arm. 'I r-really need my shield,' she stammered through chattering teeth. 'It's so c-cold.'

Loki laughed as snow filled the air, landing on Fenrir's fur, covering him in white spots.

'What are you doing?' Hel spluttered. She shook Loki's arm. 'This is my kingdom; you can't just mess about with it.'

'Shut up, Hel,' Vali shouted. 'No one cares about your rotten kingdom!'

Hel spun towards him, her needle teeth snarling. 'STOP INSULTING MY HOME!'

Fenrir growled.

Vali staggered as the ground beneath him turned soft and boggy, his stone feet sinking into the earth.

Whetstone and Lotta wobbled, the soil soupy under their feet.

'What's happening?' Whetstone yelled as the snow

thickened and the ground sucked at his boots. Fenrir yelped as his paws sank.

'This is Hel's kingdom,' Lotta called back as Vali struggled to free himself. 'She can control everything. She's turned the ground into quicksand!'

'You've got him, Hel.' Loki laughed as Vali sank up to his knees, his own boots balancing on top of the spongy ground. 'Now finish him off!'

Whetstone and Lotta ducked as Vali sent a blast of green magic towards his sister. Lightning crackled along her bones, sparks leaping between her needle teeth.

She shrieked and the ground turned solid again. Loki cackled with glee, relishing the destruction.

'Get up!' Whetstone tried to pull Lotta onwards. 'Quick, while they're all distracted.'

'I can't. My boots – I'm stuck.' Lotta's heavy armoured boots had sunk into the now solid quicksand. She fumbled to undo them.

Flashes of darkness filled the field as Hel hurled balls of black fire at her brother. Whetstone flinched when Lotta touched his arm. They crawled away, her abandoned boots sticking out of the ground. Fenrir threw his head back and howled, his fur caked in mud.

'That's enough!' Loki bellowed, stepping between his son and daughter. 'Focus on the boy – don't let him get away.'

Hel turned to look for Whetstone, a fireball still in her skeleton hand.

With a huge effort, Vali wrenched his feet out of the earth. Cracks opened across the ground, which quickly filled with snow. His clothes were covered with charred spots where Hel's fire had struck him. He yanked a knife out of his belt and flicked it towards his sister.

The movement caught Hel's eye. The fireball vanished and she grabbed a nearby cheerleader, pulling it in front of her as a shield. The knife hit the Helhest and disappeared with a faint *gloop*. Hel bared her teeth in a snarl and gestured towards Vali.

'Look out!' Whetstone yelled as the Helhest rose behind Vali.

Hod had said the Helhest fed on the spirts of dead Vikings and that touching it for too long would be deadly. Vali darted forward, grabbing his sister in a bear hug and lifting her off her feet, her arms trapped by her sides. Hel shrieked and bit into Vali's shoulder with her needle teeth. Bone squealed against stone. The Helhest swept over both of them like a tide. Fenrir yelped and pawed at their struggling forms.

Whetstone guided the violently trembling Valkyrie away from the battling siblings, trying to keep one eye on Loki through the whirling snow. 'Stay here. It's too dangerous.'

'You're h-having a laugh.' Lotta pushed past Whetstone, propelling herself into the snowstorm, desperate for her shield. 'The challenge is still on. We can win this.'

Chapter Eighteen

Cats and Gods

Whetstone shook the snow out of his face. Shapes danced through the falling flakes, making it difficult to see. The boy stumbled after the Valkyrie, heading for where he had last seen the shield. A hand grabbed his ankle. Whetstone leaped into the air, instinctively kicking the hand away. He heard a human-sounding groan. 'Dad?'

Hod pushed himself into a sitting position. 'I fink you bwoke my dose.'

'Achoo!' Lotta sneezed loudly somewhere in front of them.

'Sorry, I have to get the shield!' Whetstone darted after her, leaving his father pinching his nose to try to stop the bleeding.

'Achoo! ACHOO!'

Following the sound of sneezing, Whetstone stumbled across the plain. His foot brushed against something. His fumbling fingers found a round, flat object. Lotta's shield! He pulled it upright and brushed the snow off.

'It's here!' he yelled, looking around for the Valkyrie. 'We win – I've got it!'

A flash of green light knocked him backwards, the shield

skittering out of his grasp. Whetstone shook his head, trying to clear his vision as Loki appeared out of the snowstorm. The boy scrambled towards the shield and managed to dig his fingers under the metal rim. A soft leather boot landed on the shield and pushed down, trapping his fingers.

Whetstone struggled to free his hand. 'Ow! Get off, Loki. Lotta needs this shield.'

'You should've taken my offer—'

Lotta materialized through the snow. 'LOKI, CATCH!' The cat hit Loki full in the face, knocking him down.

'Ha, just like on the longboat!' Whetstone grinned.

Lotta swayed, her chest heaving.

'Here!' Whetstone shoved the shield across the rapidly freezing ground, it skidded towards her like a lethal ice puck. Lotta dropped to her knees, collapsing across the shield.

Whetstone scuttled towards her. 'Lotta, are you OK?'

Beneath the fallen Valkyrie, the shield flickered and went dark.

Whetstone shook her shoulder. 'Lotta?'

Freyja's fluffy cat appeared out of the snow and rubbed itself against the girl's arm. Whetstone waited for the sneeze.

Loki sat up and shook the snow off his blond hair. Somewhere in the storm, a wolf howled mournfully.

'What did you do to her?' Whetstone demanded.

Loki climbed lightly to his feet, wiping blood off his face. 'I didn't have to do anything.' He kicked some snow over Lotta's unmoving body. 'The girl is dead.'

Somewhere in the distance Whetstone heard Vali give a shout. Hel's giggle rang out.

A sob rose in Whetstone's chest. Overwhelming loss crashed over him. He shook Lotta's shoulder again. She couldn't really be gone, not when they had come so far. Without Lotta he would never have found out about the harp strings, or the curse. He would never have visited other worlds or discovered that he could be a Hero. He had only done half these things because Lotta had been there, pushing him along. Whetstone balled his hands into fists, the pain in his crushed fingers a welcome distraction from the pain of losing his friend.

Loki held out a hand to Whetstone. 'Just give me the harp string and this will all be over.'

Whetstone reached into his pocket. Loki was right – where was Odin when he needed him? The glowing string tingled against his skin. He had tried, but he was only a human. He couldn't defeat someone like Loki.

Whetstone looked into the Trickster's face to see if there was any trace of a lie there. Dark eyes bored into him. Whetstone opened his mouth to speak but then a moving shape appeared in the sky above them. Loki's head snapped upward, and he spat out a curse.

Whetstone craned his neck – there *was* something up there. The shape grew larger.

Loki paced forward. 'Give the harp string to me! Now!'

Next to Lotta, Mr Tiddles stretched and purred. Dark shapes descended through the swirling snow. A pair of cats the size of bears – one grey-striped, the other black and white – landed gently on the ground, their paws not breaking through the snow, but skimming softly on top of it. Whetstone was so busy staring at the enormous cats that he almost didn't notice the chariot. A dark-skinned woman jumped down and marched towards them, her fluffy slippers crunching through the snow.

Whetstone's mouth went dry. He shoved the harp string back into his pocket. 'Fre-Freyja?'

The snowy wind tugged at her fur-lined cloak, pushing down her hood, which Whetstone noticed had fabric cat ears sewn on to it. Round her neck, a golden necklace glowed brightly. Her eyes flashed impossibly brighter and her mouth was set in a grim line. She was beautiful in the way a fire was beautiful: dazzling – and dangerous.

Fenrir prowled through the snow, growling. One of the giant cats hissed at him in return.

'WHERE. IS. MY. CAT?'

Whetstone grabbed Mr Tiddles from where Lotta lay and held it out to the woman. Freyja snatched the cat and cradled it like a baby. 'Mr Tiddles! Mummy has missed you!' The cat clawed her affectionately as the woman cooed.

Whetstone's fingers twisted together. 'What about Lotta? Can you help her, please?'

The woman peered down at the trainee Valkyrie lying half hidden in the snow. 'She got her shield back, then, I see.'

Hope blossomed in Whetstone's chest. Freyja was supposed

to have powerful magic. Perhaps even more powerful than Loki. If anyone could help Lotta, it would be Freyja.

Freyja frowned. 'Valkyries are more Odin's department.' She glanced at something over Whetstone's shoulder. 'Loki. I might have guessed I'd find you here.' Her nose scrunched up as if a bad smell had wafted beneath it; Mr Tiddles meowed.

'Looking lovely as ever, Freyja,' Loki said with a small bow. 'Found your cat, then?'

'No thanks to you.'

Loki grinned. 'Believe it or not, taking your cat had nothing to do with me.'

'This time.'

Loki dipped his head in acknowledgement. 'I'm surprised to see you here. I thought Glinting-Fire had stopped anyone leaving Asgard.'

Freyja raised an eyebrow. 'And how would you know that?'

A thin figure appeared at Loki's side. Freyja pulled her cloak in round her shoulders. 'Hello, Hel.'

'You can get lost, Freyja. We don't need your sort here,' Hel snarled through her needle teeth.

Freyja tossed back her hair; the golden threads twisted through it bringing a hint of summer to the snowy field. 'Gladly.' She tucked the cat into the chariot and picked up the reins.

'Have a safe trip back to Asgard.' Loki smirked. 'Lovely of you to visit.'

'Wait!' Whetstone grabbed the side of the chariot. 'Take us with you. Me and Lotta. We saved your cat.' The woman turned as Whetstone circled the chariot, avoiding Loki. 'Odin sent me on a quest. You need to take us back to Asgard.'

'You'll be lucky,' Loki snorted. 'The lovely Freyja isn't exactly known for her hospitality.'

Freyja glared. 'I can be perfectly hospitable, just not with people who keep trying to sell me to the Giants for their own benefit.'

'Take the girl, then.' Loki made a grab for Whetstone. 'That boy is mine.'

'No, that boy is yours.' Freyja pointed

through the snow to where Vali stood. A few chips had been knocked out of him and a long crack ran down the side of his face, making his resemblance to Loki stronger than ever. Hel snarled.

'You really did turn him to stone?' Freyja said in surprise, stepping out of the chariot and touching her brown fingers to Vali's grey cheek. 'Does your mother know about this? You can't just turn back, you know.'

Loki raised a hand full of green light. 'I told you to *go*, Freyja.'

Whetstone gritted his teeth, waiting for Loki to use the magic.

But, instead, everything stopped.

A huge beam of light lit up the battlefield. Through slitted lids, Whetstone managed to make out snowflakes hanging motionless in the air. He turned his head, searching for the source of the brightness. It was Lotta's shield.

With a soft *poof*, all the snowflakes turned into feathers and spiralled gently to the ground. The light faded. Whetstone stood, stunned, ankle-deep in a drift of fluff.

With a groan, Lotta pushed herself upright, feathers sticking crazily out of her black curls. They all watched in silence as, pulling her shield on to her arm, she slowly got to her feet. 'What happened?'

'Good question.' Whetstone twitched as plumes found their way in through holes in his clothes and tickled his white skin.

Freyja stepped through the downy drifts. 'Are you all right?' She peered into Lotta's confused face. 'How are you feeling?'

Behind Lotta, the dark shape of Fenrir jumped into piles of feathers, barking with delight.

'A bit lightheaded, I guess.'

A chuckle bubbled out of Whetstone's mouth: relief, shock and happiness that Lotta was OK all rolled together. For a second, he even thought about hugging her, but quickly changed his mind. Maybe not mid-battle. 'What's with all the feathers?'

Lotta looked around herself in amazement. 'Did I do that? Feathers usually only appear when I transform . . .'

Hel stamped her foot. 'You FREAK! Helheim is *filled* with feathers. What next – flowers? Sunshine? PICNICS?' Behind her, Vali grinned broadly.

Freyja carefully looked Lotta up and down. 'We're

leaving. Get on the chariot, you two.'

Loki crossed his arms. 'I don't think so.'

Freyja glared. 'And whose army is going to stop me? Yours?'

'No.' Loki grinned. 'Hers.'

Beside him, Hel's face had gone white with fury. She threw back her head and released an inhuman scream into the sky. All around her the drifts of feathers burst into wraiths of grey smoke. Freyja's giant cats hissed and spat as the ground beneath their paws shuddered.

The Helhest surged forward. Vali leaped out of the way of the glistening tide. It surrounded Freyja, Whetstone and Lotta in a wide ring before swelling upwards, turning into heavily armed cheerleaders, *Hel's Belles Armed Battalion* embroidered on their uniforms. Mr Tiddles clawed his way on to the side of the chariot and hissed at them.

'At Ragnarok the Helhest will rise,' Hel spat. 'Swarming

over the Nine Worlds and bringing about the end of the Gods.'

'It's not Ragnarok yet, sweetie,' Freyja replied unfazed, blowing a kiss and stepping gracefully into the chariot.

Whetstone jumped up behind Freyja and reached down to help Lotta up. Instead, the trainee Valkyrie faced the Hel's Belles and pulled out the rusty sword, which glowed with a new silvery light.

'It didn't do that before.' Lotta whacked a nearby cheerleader, who crumbled to dust. 'It didn't do that either.'

Loki gave a whistle. All heads turned to where he now stood next to the huge cats. 'Don't make me hurt them, Freyja,' he said sadly. Green sparks leaped from his fingers. The giant tabby hissed.

Freyja's beautiful face curved into a snarl. 'Touch one whisker and I'll end you.'

Loki grinned. Hel's army marched forward, tightening their circle. 'The only way out is up. Why risk the extra weight? Take the cat and leave the kids.'

Vali put his hand on his sister's arm. 'Hel, let them go. Call off the Helhest.' Two of the cheerleaders grabbed him. He struggled, but might as well have been trying to fight a river.

Green light crackled, but before Loki could do anything, Hod's strong arms caught him from behind, pinning his arms to his sides.

'Dad!' Whetstone lunged over the side of the chariot, desperate to reach his father. Lotta stepped into the chariot, trapping Whetstone inside.

'Get out of here!' Hod called, struggling to keep hold of

Loki, who was transforming into different animals, trying to free himself. A snake, a fish, a bird . . . 'Take the harp string and go!'

Whetstone looked hopelessly at Lotta. They couldn't go, not like this. Guilt at almost forgetting about his father surged through him. He had come to Helheim to try and reunite his family and now he was expected to leave his dad behind. 'I can't. I—' He tried to push past the Valkyrie.

Lotta clapped a hand over his mouth, shoving him back. 'GO!' she screamed at Freyja, who cracked the reins. The two enormous cats leaped into the air, pulling the chariot and its occupants into the sky.

Whetstone tugged Lotta's hands off his face. 'We have to go back.'

'Hel was right about one thing: Heroes have to make tough choices. We have to get the harp string away from Loki,' Lotta said firmly, keeping hold of

235

the struggling boy. 'We need to leave before Hel turns those cheerleaders into giant eagles or dragons or . . . *something*.'

A screech echoed from below them. Dark shapes swirled. Freyja urged the cats higher. 'Why did you have to think of that?' she muttered.

Above them hung the red dome of Helheim's sky. Whetstone closed his eyes as they passed through it and out into the roots of Yggdrasil, the shrieks of Helheim drifting into silence.

Lotta peered over the edge of the chariot, watching as Helheim rapidly vanished below them. 'Shame. I was just getting used to the place,' she said, releasing Whetstone.

'Sometimes being a Hero is really rubbish.' Whetstone massaged his jaw where Lotta had gripped him. 'If I was an ordinary person, I could've taken Loki's offer and gone back to Midgard with my dad.'

'And Loki would've opened the walls between the worlds, and you'd be flattened by a Giant,' Lotta pointed out. She smoothed her black curls, watching him. 'We'll get him back – your dad. I promise. And Vali – we'll get him too,' she added. 'He was pretty useful in the end.'

Whetstone nodded and rubbed his eyes. 'I got the harp string, but lost my dad. Again. It really is the Land of Lost Things.' A hard lump formed in his throat, making it hard to speak. Who knew what Loki and Hel might be doing to his dad now?

Something rattled inside his boot. Whetstone tugged it off his foot and a charm in the shape of a fish fell out. He pulled the harp string out of his pocket. No longer shining to warn of danger, it sat on his palm, faded and dull. He threaded the charm on to it before tying it round his neck.

One down, two to go.

Whetstone rubbed his face. He blinked, trying to distract himself from the hollowness inside. 'What happened back there? You know, the feathers and the sword and everything?'

Lotta shrugged. 'I dunno. I felt kind of weird.'

Despite himself, Whetstone sniggered.

'What?'

'Lotta, you literally turned a snowstorm into feathers. I'd say that was more than a bit weird.' He looked at her carefully. 'You said the feathers only appeared when you transformed, but you're not currently a bird?'

'Thanks for noticing.'

Behind them Freyja snorted.

Lotta carefully pulled out the rusty sword and held it in front of her, Whetstone leaning out of the way to avoid the long blade. Lotta swung the sword towards him. Silver beads appeared along the notched edge.

Whetstone reached out to touch one. 'Well, you *are* a dodgy Valkyrie, so I guess it makes sense that you've got a dodgy sword.'

'I wouldn't do that,' said Freyja, not taking her eyes off the giant cats as they followed the trunk of Yggdrasil towards Muspell and Svartalfheim. 'We need to get Eir, Goddess of Healing, to take a look at you, Lotta. I think something has gone a bit wrong.'

Lotta lowered the sword and looked at Whetstone nervously. He shrugged, not knowing what to say.

Lotta slid the sword back into its scabbard. 'Are things bad in Asgard?'

Freyja nodded. 'Not just Asgard.'

The smell of rotten eggs filled the air as they soared past the smouldering world of Muspell. Red sparks drifted towards them, leaving soot marks on the sides of the chariot. Whetstone peered over the side. 'Muspell looks the same.'

With a hiccup, a cascade of Loki-like green sparks shot out of one of the volcanos. Whetstone leaned back. 'Green magic? That can't be good.'

'The Dwarves are quiet,' Lotta remarked, pointing towards the mines and mountains which made up Svartalfheim. Red light glinted out of cracks and doorways, but there was no movement.

'Glinting-Fire has put in a big order,' Freyja replied. 'She needs more weapons for her army.'

'*Her* army?' Lotta repeated dumbly.

'We'll be back in Asgard in no time,' Freyja announced as they climbed higher and higher. Whetstone's ears went *pop*. 'Then you can see for yourself.'

❆

The chariot rocked gently as the flying cats pounded through the branches of the world tree, reminding Whetstone of the movement of the longboat. He sank on to the floor and rested his head against the wooden side. Giant cats were *almost* better than horses at pulling chariots. Whetstone wondered if it would catch on but thought that trying to get two cats to go in the same direction at the same time couldn't be easy. Maybe it only worked if you had Freyja's magic powers.

The mountainous world of the Giants emerged from Yggdrasil's branches. Whetstone gazed at the snow-covered landscape and shivered. It reminded him too much of Helheim. He wondered what Odin was up to down there, and if he knew what was going on.

Lotta sat beside him, chewing her thumbnail. 'But *why* does Glinting-Fire need an army?' she asked for the thousandth time. 'Is it something to do with the training camps?'

Freyja gave a tense smile.

At last, Asgard, Home of the Gods, arose in front of them. It sat on a grassy island on the topmost branches of Yggdrasil. Whetstone had never seen Asgard from the outside before as he had been unconscious when Lotta had accidentally brought him there the last time. His mouth fell open in astonishment.

Huge white walls surrounded the city. They blazed in the sunlight, making it look as if Asgard was protected by a ring of fire. Carved deeply into the mighty walls were the words:

FROST GIANTS KEEP OUT

Underneath and heavily crossed out was:

~~Loki smels of poOo~~

Whetstone found himself smiling.

The cats circled the white walls before landing lightly in front of a pair of enormous and heavily barred gates. Freyja pointed a ring-laden finger at the gates and a jet of red light shot out of her hand. The gates swung open.

'Wait, you don't need a key?' Lotta exclaimed. 'That's so unfair!'

Freyja smiled. 'Glinting-Fire certainly thinks so.' Her eyebrows drew together; she lowered her voice. 'You two had better hide. As you know, living humans

aren't usually welcome in Asgard, and I think it's best if Glinting-Fire doesn't know you're back, Lotta.'

The boy and trainee Valkyrie ducked down, pulling Freyja's fur-lined cloak, which had been discarded in the bottom of the chariot, over their heads.

'Go away, Mr Tiddles!' Lotta hissed as the cat squeezed in beside them.

The giant cats purred as they stalked in through the gates. A pair of Valkyries on guard duty struggled against magical red ropes. Freyja clicked her fingers to free them, but didn't stop.

Despite his sorrow at leaving his dad in Helheim, and his fear of being caught, Whetstone couldn't resist peeking out to see if Asgard was as amazing as he remembered. The giant cats picked their way through the streets, crowds of glowing people parting before them. Ravens swooped through the air. Magnificent houses, each the size of the Great Hall in Krud, lined the paths, different silver emblems displayed on their doors to show which God lived where.

Whetstone shuddered as they passed a low, dark house decorated with snakes: Loki's house. The shutters were closed and no smoke came from the chimney. Beside him, Lotta held her nose and stifled a sneeze.

Whetstone's stomach rumbled at the smell of roasting meat as they approached Valhalla, its towering walls of spears and shields looming over the rest of Asgard.

Lotta stuck her head out as they rounded a corner and the Valkyrie training school swung into view. Her mouth dropped open. 'What is *that*?'

Gone was the battered *Valkyrie Training School* sign. Now, bright flags hung from the walls. Symbols Whetstone recognized from the different Gods' houses decorated some of the flags. He wasn't surprised to see Loki's snakes prominently in view. In the centre was a blood-red flag with a picture of a raven holding a warrior in its claws.

'She's got all the shields,' Lotta whispered in a shaking voice. 'Look.' In the centre of the courtyard and guarded by Flee and Flay was a large shield rack filled with dozens of circular glowing shields. All nailed in place and encased in magical green ice.

'I remember that ice stuff,' Whetstone hissed. 'It's what Loki used to trap Flee and Flay.'

'It must be how Glinting-Fire is controlling the Valkyries.'

'Good thing she hasn't got your shield, then.'

Lotta ran her fingers lovingly over the splintery shield wedged in beside her.

Valkyries jogged out of the courtyard to block Freyja's path. Among them Lotta recognized Akrid with her distinctive dreadlocks. All the Valkyries now had eyes the same shade of green as the ice. One of Freyja's giant cats hissed at the interruption. The other cat sat down to wash itself, making the chariot tilt drunkenly to the side. Whetstone pulled Freyja's cloak back over their heads.

'What's going on?' Freyja lifted her chin as the Valkyries lined up in front of her.

The rows parted as Glinting-Fire stepped forward, her clipboard clenched tightly in her hand. 'You shouldn't have done that to my guard-Valkyries, Freyja. You know Odin, or one of his assistants – me – has to approve any trips out of Asgard.'

Freyja fixed the tattooed Valkyrie with a scowl. 'You are not in charge of Asgard, and you are certainly not in charge of me. Odin will return from Jotunheim and stop this nonsense soon enough.'

Whetstone peeped out. A crowd of onlookers had gathered behind the chariot, trapping them. Mr Tiddles rubbed up against Lotta, who held her nose. Whetstone grimaced at her – she couldn't sneeze now!

Glinting-Fire walked round the chariot. Whetstone and Lotta held their breath as the short Valkyrie tapped the chariot with her pencil. 'Have you given any more thought to my offer, Freyja?'

Freyja pulled herself up to her full height on the wonky chariot. 'I wouldn't join you for all the warriors in Midgard,' she announced. 'And those who do join you are fools,' she added loudly.

Glinting-Fire sniffed and scribbled something on her clipboard. 'How disappointing. Many others have seen the light and joined our cause. You will change your mind in time. You like a Hero, don't you, Freyja?'

Someone in the crowd laughed. Freyja swung round to glare at them.

'But where has she been?' called Flee from her position guarding the shields. 'She hasn't said.'

Glinting-Fire nodded. 'Well, Freyja? We're all ears.'

Freyja drew in a breath. 'I finally found my cat, if you must know.' She fumbled under the cloak for Mr Tiddles. Lotta let go of her nose as the cat was lifted out.

Glinting-Fire narrowed her eyes. 'How interesting. Where was he – Midgard? Helheim?'

Peering through a gap in the cloak, Whetstone saw Flee and Flay glance at each other.

A clump of cat hair wafted past Lotta's face.

Freyja tossed her twists. 'No. Niflheim.'

Flee and Flay sighed with relief.

Lotta squeezed her nose again, her eyes tight shut. Whetstone clutched her arm, mouthing, '*No!*'

'Now if you don't mind,' Freyja said as her giant cats stretched and stood up, 'I need to give Mr Tiddles a bath—'

Lotta gave an enormous sneeze. 'ACHOO!'

'– because I think he's caught a cold,' Freyja finished quickly. She jiggled the reins and the cats moved forward, shouldering their way through the ranks of green-eyed Valkyries.

Lotta wiped her nose on her shoulder and smiled apologetically.

'The Nine Worlds are shifting!' Glinting-Fire called after them. 'The old order will be replaced. Join us and rise or stand against us and fall!'

Lotta glanced at Whetstone. 'She sounds like Loki,' she whispered, her fingers squeezing her shield tightly.

Whetstone nodded. 'We stopped Loki and we can stop her too.' He gripped Lotta's arm. 'Look at what we've done already. I got the first harp string, and you got your shield back, *and* you're not under Glinting-Fire's power like the others.'

Lotta smiled a bit.

Whetstone grinned. 'You're a Valkyrie. I'm a Hero. The Nine Worlds depend on us – what could go wrong?'

Keep reading for more fun
in the Nine Worlds!

Whetstone left these scraps of paper behind in Krud.
Maybe you can help Awfulrick make sense of them.

Angrboda's Terrifying Tales for Tiny Tots
A Journey to Helheim

Once upon a time, a great Chief decided to visit Helheim. This was a very stupid idea as you will see. He wanted to visit the spirit of a powerful fortune teller, which was pointless as his future would now be to stay in Helheim with the dead forever and ever and ever.

Anyway, the stupid Chief set off on his journey. To reach Helheim he travelled nine days north and down until he found himself in a strange country where herbs grew in winter. Some herbs anyway. Deadly nightshade, Mandrakes, Wormwood and Henbane . . . Poisonous ones, you get the idea.

After crossing through the herbs, the Chief reached a fast-flowing river filled with shattered weapons. The only way across the river was over a shining golden bridge. The bridge is guarded by a monster whose job

*Forever?
Gulp*

How do you travel nine days down? Do I have to dig a tunnel?

*Remember:
Don't eat the green stuff.
I'm poor and I've given myself food, does that count?
Better bring a cake just in case.*

IT IS TO MAKE SURE NO ONE LEAVES HELHEIM. THE
CHIEF SAFELY PASSED THE MONSTER AND MET HEL'S
DOG - A REAL HEL HOUND, TO WHOM YOU HAVE TO
FEED HEL CAKE. LUCKILY FOR THE CHIEF, HE HAD
GIVEN FOOD TO THE POOR DURING HIS LIFETIME
AND A HEL CAKE APPEARED, SO HE WASN'T EATEN BY
THE DOG.

NEXT CAME THE DESERTED BATTLEFIELD WHERE
THE FIGHTERS HAD LONG SINCE GIVEN UP, AND
THEN THE EMPTY SNOW FIELDS AND DULL VILLAGES.
THIS IS WHERE THE DEAD WAIT UNTIL RAGNAROK
WHEN THEY WILL RISE UP AND JOIN HEL IN THE
GLORIOUS FIGHT AGAINST THE GODS. FINALLY, IN
THE DISTANCE A GREAT HALL APPEARED. THIS IS THE
HOME OF HEL, THE MAGNIFICENT QUEEN OF THE
DEAD.

BUT THE STUPID CHIEF DID NOT WISH TO
VISIT HEL - HE WANTED TO FIND THIS FORTUNE
TELLER. UNFORTUNATELY FOR THE CHIEF, THE DEAD
CANNOT SPEAK TO THE LIVING, SO HIS JOURNEY
WAS POINTLESS. YOU WOULD THINK HE WOULD HAVE
CHECKED THIS OUT BEFORE GOING ALL THAT WAY.
AS FAR AS I KNOW HE'S STILL THERE NOW, TRAPPED
ALL ALONE WITH THE SPIRITS OF THE DEAD IN THE
FROZEN LAND OF THE LOST. FOREVER.

SWEET DREAMS.

If the
monster's
only job is
to stop people
leaving, I
should be
able to get
into Helheim
no problem.

Snow fields?
I might
need extra
socks.
Maybe my
dad will be
in one of
the villages?

So how am
I going
to get out
again with
my dad?

Can you help Lotta fill in this form by writing in some examples of how she has used her Valkyrie skills?

Valkyrie Report Feedback Form

Please provide evidence for how you think you have demonstrated the following skills:

	Score
Fighting:	%
Horse Riding:	%

I successfully rode Thighbiter to Midgard on several occasions. He always has a very clean stable and I am working on stopping him from biting me so much.

	Score
Epic Poetry:	%
Transforming into Swans:	%
Serving Mead in Valhalla:	%

I can carry three jugs of mead at once without spilling any all of it.

Collecting Fallen Warriors:	%

I am so good at this I can collect warriors before they're fallen. This is a good thing, honest.

Why not recreate your favourite scene from the Land of Lost Things with your very own Helhest! Make sure you check with a grown-up first.

DIY Helhest

Ingredients:
100ml PVA glue
Black food colouring (gel is best)
Contact-lens solution
1tsp bicarbonate of soda
An adult to assist

Instructions:
1. Add 1tsp bicarbonate of soda to 100ml PVA glue. Stir until fully mixed.
2. Add food colouring to the mixture a drop at a time and stir until it is dark and menacing.
3. Mix in small amounts of contact-lens solution. Keep stirring until it forms slimy strands.
4. Teach it to obey your every whim and take over the Nine Worlds!

Return your Helhest to a lidded pot or zip-lock bag when not in use to keep it fresh.
Be careful it doesn't stain your hands, clothes or enemies.

TOP TRUMPS

Out of all the monsters and animals we have met so far, who do you think would win in a battle?

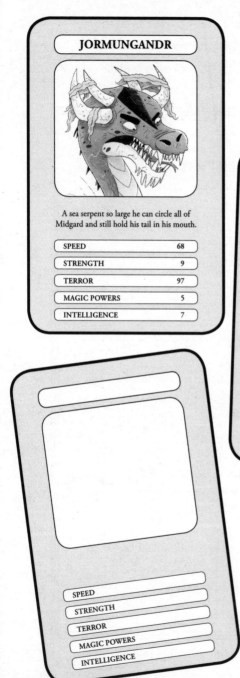

JORMUNGANDR

A sea serpent so large he can circle all of Midgard and still hold his tail in his mouth.

SPEED	68
STRENGTH	9
TERROR	97
MAGIC POWERS	5
INTELLIGENCE	7

FENRIR

An enormous wolf who likes tummy rubs.

SPEED	57
STRENGTH	8
TERROR	63
MAGIC POWERS	4
INTELLIGENCE	6

SPEED	
STRENGTH	
TERROR	
MAGIC POWERS	
INTELLIGENCE	

Or invent your own monster and beat them all. Will it be a wolf, a snake, a bird or something else? Fill in this card, and remember to give your monster a terrifying name!

THIGHBITER

Lotta's troublesome flying warhorse.

SPEED	71
STRENGTH	7
TERROR	45
MAGIC POWERS	7
INTELLIGENCE	6

NIDHOGG

The dragon from Niflheim who likes to terrorize the unworthy dead.

SPEED	71
STRENGTH	7
TERROR	45
MAGIC POWERS	7
INTELLIGENCE	6

MR TIDDLES

Freyja's favourite cat. Huge and fluffy with a face like a furry fist.

SPEED	71
STRENGTH	7
TERROR	45
MAGIC POWERS	7
INTELLIGENCE	6

HELHEST

Dark and sticky it can take any form and serves Hel, Queen of the Dead.

SPEED	64
STRENGTH	7
TERROR	95
MAGIC POWERS	9
INTELLIGENCE	5

Norse God or Goddess Name Generator

Vikings had hundreds of Gods and Goddesses.
Use the name generator to find out which
Norse God or Goddess you could be.

First letter of your last name:

Aegir or Alfa	Njord or Nanna
Baldr or Beyla	Otta or Odr
Cante or Cara	Porg or Pri
Dagmar or Dor	Querd or Quindr
Eir or Embala	Raan or Rig
Forseti or Fulla	Sif or Skirnir
Gefion or Grimnir	Tyr or Thiazi
Hermod or Hati	Urd or Ullr
Idunn or Irpa	Vili or Var
Jarl or Jorth	Woland or Wrigga
Kvasir or Kara	Xeidr or Xirna
Lodurr or Lif	Ymir or Yinga
Mimir or Modi	Zisa or Zven

Favourite colour:	God/dess of:	Birth Month:	Animal Companion:
Red	Feasting	January	Wolf
Orange	Battle	February	Bear
Yellow	Travel	March	Horse
Green	Weather	April	Snake
Blue	Nature	May	Cat
Purple	Friendship	June	Dragon
Pink	Success	July	Goat
Black	Healing	August	Raven
White	Water	September	Dolphin
Brown	Animals	October	Eagle
Silver	Fire	November	Deer
Gold	Magic	December	Otter

There are five Viking runes hidden in the illustrations throughout the book. Find them and use the translator below to solve the riddle and unlock the first chapter of:

A GATHERING OF GIANTS

The Nine Worlds are shifting and shaking;
Whetstone and Lotta are in hiding together.
To find the last two magic harp strings,
Freyja will loan Whetstone this made of falcon feathers.

What am I?

☐ ☐ ☐ ☐ ☐

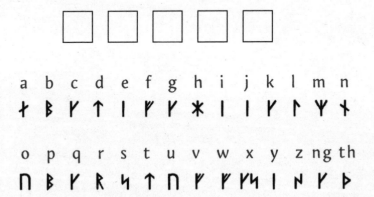

a	b	c	d	e	f	g	h	i	j	k	l	m	n

o	p	q	r	s	t	u	v	w	x	y	z	ng	th

Chapter One

A Birthday to Remember

'I look ridiculous!'

Whetstone peered at himself in the polished bronze mirror. His reflection was a bit wobbly and blurred, but he could see enough. That was the thing about staying with Freyja, the Goddess of Love and Sorcery: there were plenty of reflective surfaces. 'I feel like an idiot.' He pushed the feather, which stuck out of his hat, away from his eye. Gone were his scruffy clothes with their familiar holes and patches, replaced by . . . *this*.

Lotta's face contorted as she forced down a grin. 'It's not *that* bad.'

Whetstone twirled around. The sky-blue woollen tunic and leather belt were alright, even if the fur trim itched against his neck. But the trousers were just stupid. Big and baggy and pleated with green and white stripes, they ballooned out around his legs before being pulled in tight just below his knees. Strips of fabric wound snugly around his calves to finish the look. Lotta's eyes bulged as she tried not to laugh.

'I don't see why Freyja won't let us wear our own clothes,' Whetstone moaned as he tightened his belt, worried his saggy breeches might slip down at any moment.

'Because we're fugitives in Asgard and we don't want anyone to recognize us?' Lotta suggested. Asgard was the home of the Gods and a very dangerous place for a living human and disgraced trainee Valkyrie to be hiding.

'Recognize YOU, you mean. No one knows me!' Whetstone pouted. 'Why do I have to look like a fool?'

'Yeah, no one knows you – except most of the Valkyries, and Loki, and—'

'Loki isn't back in Asgard yet.'

'*Yet.*' Lotta nudged Whetstone out of the way of the mirror. Instead of her usual leather and armour, she was wearing a pair of loose silk trousers and an embroidered tunic that contrasted perfectly with her brown skin, her black hair tucked neatly away beneath a patterned head wrap. She scratched at her head. 'I can't decide if it's a good thing he's not back yet, or if it just means he's planning something really bad.' The last time Whetstone and Lotta had seen Loki, he'd tracked them to Helheim, one of the most miserable places in the Nine Worlds.

'*And* you didn't have to have a B A T H,' Whetstone muttered, his skin looking pinker and cleaner than it had in a long time. The feather flicked back into his eye. 'I can't think of many things worse than a bath.'

Behind them, a string of bunting was hoisted up

towards the gold domed ceiling. '*I* can't believe Freyja is actually going ahead with this party,' Lotta muttered, straightening her tunic.

'It's her birthday, it would look weird if she didn't,' Whetstone replied, stepping out of the way of a servant boy unenthusiastically pushing a broom across the floor.

Party preparations continued around them. Rich tapestries and brightly woven fabrics decorated the walls of Freyja's Great Hall. A long table had been pushed to one side and clusters of chairs were dotted around the space. Another servant scampered about lighting clay lamps.

A very large and fluffy brown cat watched the servants scurry to and fro, his eyes on the bowls of nibbles they carried. With a leap, the cat landed on the long table, sending plates and glasses flying. Whetstone dashed across the room and snatched the cat up around the middle. 'Stop it, Mr Tiddles. You're going to get in trouble.'

The cat gave Whetstone a grumpy look as the boy carried him across the room to his bed of plump cushions. Lotta pinched her nose as they passed to try and hold back a sneeze. She was explosively allergic to cats.

With a screech which almost made Whetstone drop the cat, a coppery falcon swooped into the room. In a ripple of light, the falcon transformed into Freyja, the birthday girl herself. A vision in silks and gold, she unfastened a feathery cloak and handed it to a waiting servant. Her magic necklace gleamed against the brown skin of her throat. She turned to Whetstone and Lotta. 'There you two are!'

Whetstone dropped Mr Tiddles onto his cushion and moved to face her, his bottom lip sticking out. He gestured at his clothes. 'Why? Why would you make me wear this?'

Freyja straightened the feathery plumes on his hat. 'You're hiding in plain sight. The last place anyone would think to look for you is with the musicians.'

Lotta let out a snort of laughter.

'Musicians?' Whetstone spluttered. 'But I'm not musical: I can't play any instruments or anything!'

'It's simple. Just hang around at the back of the group and look busy,' Freyja handed him a narrow, wooden harp.

Whetstone took it sourly, 'A harp? You think you're funny, don't you?'

Whetstone's problems had begun when he and his parents had got in the way of Loki stealing a magic harp from the Dwarves. The Dwarves had cursed the harp strings, hiding them in separate worlds so that Loki would be unable to use their power. As Whetstone and his parents had been holding the strings at the time, they were taken along with the strings and separated. Now, Loki was hunting down the missing harp strings. Not to reunite Whetstone's broken family or to make amends for his theft, but to use the powers they contained. Odin had set Whetstone the quest of collecting the strings before

Loki could take them. A quest which had led them across several of the Nine Worlds before finally ending up here, at Freyja's birthday party.

Lotta bit her lip. 'Freyja, are you sure this is a good idea? Most of Asgard is coming to this party. Maybe it would be better if we just hid somewhere.'

'No way!' Whetstone spluttered. 'I've been looking forward to this. I want to know what happens at a Goddess' party.'

'You'll be safer out in the open,' Freyja explained. 'My last party got a bit out of control. I found Thor snoring in my wardrobe the next morning. Plus no one really looks at servants.'

Lotta crossed her arms.

'It will be fine.' Freyja picked up a platter of tiny sandwiches. 'Just keep busy and no one will notice a thing.'

Lotta ducked through the crowd, trying to avoid catching anyone's eye, her tiny sandwiches already having been demolished by Thor in one massive mouthful. A table covered with birthday presents sat off to one side, most of them wrapped in gold paper. Lotta dawdled in front of them. Pretending to be Freyja's servant was exhausting. All of Asgard had come to the party, except for the two people she most wanted to see – Odin, the chief of the Gods, and Scold, the ex-leader of the Valkyries.

Lotta was a trainee Valkyrie, or, rather, she had been.

She wasn't quite sure what she was any more.

Valkyries were elite female warriors, brought to life by the breath of Odin and given the task of collecting fallen Heroes and warriors from the battlefields of Midgard, the human world. Unfortunately, on her first visit to Midgard, Lotta had accidentally picked up Whetstone, a very-much-alive apprentice thief instead of a dead warrior. It was only after Whetstone had proved he was a Hero after all, that Odin had allowed Lotta to continue with her Valkyrie training. But that had all happened while Scold was in charge. Things were very different with the Valkyries now.

A conga line led by Freyr, the God of Summer, danced past Lotta. Freyr was Freyja's brother, his blond hair standing out like a halo against his dark brown skin. 'La, la, la, la, la, hey!' the dancers chanted, looping around the hall and scooping up more people.

Lotta shuffled the birthday gifts around. Cat ornaments, mugs with cat ears and cat-shaped jewellery, appeared under her distracted fingers.

Whetstone had vanished into the group of musicians, all dressed in identical feathery hats and sky-blue robes. Lotta wondered what he'd told them to explain why he couldn't play the harp he was holding. Maybe they didn't care. No one seemed to have noticed that Whetstone wasn't glowing like the other inhabitants of Asgard either, so maybe Freyja had performed some magic to keep him safe.

All the room's attention was focused on Freyja, magnificent in deep-red robes. Gold jewellery flashed at her throat and wrists and the Goddess glittered like the entire contents of a gold mine had been dumped on her head.

Lotta straightened her shoulders. She *should* go back to the kitchen for more tiny sandwiches before anyone got suspicious. Instead, she pushed a few more presents into line. A stout, gold object peeked out from behind a collection of paw-print bath towels.

Lotta sucked in a breath, her heart racing. 'Oh no, not you!'

The cup jumped through the presents, landing with a clang in front of her. Lotta glanced over her shoulder and lowered her voice, 'What are you doing here?'

'I could ask you the same question.' The cup stared up at her with its ruby eyes. Lotta had borrowed the golden cup from Viking Chief Awfulrick to help her win a poetry contest. 'You told Awfulrick you were going to bring me back to Midgard over a month ago. But I'm still here!'

'I'm sorry,' Lotta retorted. 'I've been a bit busy saving the Nine Worlds. I haven't made it back to Midgard yet.'

The cup spun on the table, its squeaky voice cutting through the music. Lotta made a grab for it but missed. 'I like being back in Asgard. I think Frigg missed me.'

Lotta peered over her shoulder, searching the crowd for the Goddess of Family – the original owner of the cup. She was deep in conversation with a short woman whose dark plaits stuck out either side of her head. Lotta flinched in shock and without thinking, dived under the table. The cup jumped down to join her. 'What are you doing?'

'That's Glinting-Fire,' Lotta mumbled. Her knuckles cracked as she clenched her hands into fists, barely containing her anger. 'I can't let her see me.'

Glinting-Fire had tricked her way into her new position as leader of the Valkyries and had tried to get rid of Lotta by destroying her Valkyrie shield, worried that Lotta would try to stop her evil plans for "Valkyrie progress".

It hadn't worked.

'Good thinking.' The cup nodded. 'I'm sure no one will wonder why you're hiding under a table.'

'She doesn't know I'm back in Asgard,' Lotta hissed, peering out from between the table legs. What Glinting-Fire also didn't know, was that her plans had failed and that not only had Lotta been reunited with her shield, but she had also gained strange new powers in the process.

A pair of boots stopped next to the table and a smiling face appeared, looking down curiously at Lotta. 'Did you slip?' Freyr asked, offering her a hand.

'Er, I, no, I just—' Lotta stumbled as she climbed out, her face hot with embarrassment.

'Smooth,' the cup muttered.

The God of Summer regarded her carefully, his golden

eyes standing out clearly against his thick lashes. Lotta forced a smile. With a brief bow, the man returned to the dancers.

Lotta released a breath she didn't realize she'd been holding. 'This is too dangerous,' she muttered. 'Someone is going to start asking questions.'

'Questions like: where is Odin?' the cup said loudly, bouncing up onto her shoulder. 'And why hasn't he come back to Asgard?'

'I suppose,' Lotta snatched at the cup.

'I made up a poem about that – would you like to hear it?'

'No!'

The cup coughed.

'Why has Odin left Asgard?
Do you think he will send us a postcard?'

Frigg, the cup's owner, peered over Glinting-Fire's shoulder. 'What is that girl doing with my cup?' Glinting-Fire started to turn.

Panicking, Lotta threw the cup into the air. It landed with a smash in the middle of the dance floor, nearly braining Tyr, God of Justice. Eir, the Goddess of Healing, spun out of the way with quite an impressive pirouette. A stunned silence fell.

'DANCE BATTLE!' one of the musicians shouted.

All the Gods and Goddesses cheered. The musicians

started playing again as the Gods stampeded towards the floor, all trying to outdo each other with their impressive moves.

In the group of musicians, Lotta caught Whetstone's eye. He winked. Lotta gave him a thumbs-up, before heading back to the safety of the kitchens.

'Good idea,' the flute player wheezed to Whetstone. 'We don't get paid if they stop dancing.'

Whetstone nodded, his fingers slipping on the smooth frame of the harp. This party was unlike anything he had experienced in Midgard. Compared to large, sweaty men and women throwing ale around the village Hall back on Midgard, this party was the height of sophistication. He gawked as Freyr moonwalked across the floor to collect a bowl of strawberries.

'You're getting the hang of it now,' the harpist next to Whetstone said. 'Just keep a steady rhythm and try not to break any more of the strings.'

Whetstone nodded trying to focus on the music, his tongue sticking out of the corner of his mouth in concentration.

In his experience, harp strings were always trouble.

He had already managed to retrieve one of the three cursed harp strings he'd been quested to find – it had been sent to Helheim with his father. Whetstone won the harp string, but had been forced to leave his father behind. Now, for safe-keeping, he wore it like a necklace.

A small charm in the shape of a fish hung from it – it was all that was left of the beads his father had used to disguise it.

Next to him, the harpist's fingers flew across the strings, picking out an intricate melody, which was immediately drowned out by the Gods' tone-deaf singing.

Whetstone grinned as Glinting-Fire was dragged on to the dance floor. She was *not* a natural mover. Trying to keep time with his harp, Whetstone wondered what he and Lotta were going to do. They couldn't stay in Asgard forever. There was no sign of Odin coming back and wherever Loki was, Whetstone was sure he was up to no good. They had to find the next harp string before Loki got his hands on it.

Loki knew that Frigg's magic cup had given Whetstone a riddle to help him find the harp strings, and his missing parents. That was why Loki was so determined to hunt Whetstone down. The second part of the riddle ran through Whetstone's mind in time to the music.

The other you will find, bound by a glittering chain.
She is kept for her tears, they fall as golden rain.

That half of the riddle was more useless than the first. At least the first half had been a clue about where to start looking for his father. But golden tears and glittering chains? That could be anywhere! How in all of the Nine Worlds was he supposed to figure out where his mother was?

'. . . golden tears, I heard,' Thor said loudly, wiping his mouth with the back of his hand.

Whetstone nearly fell over in shock.

'That would be a thing to have – never-ending treasure. Every time she cries, you get richer.'

'Who told you about it?' asked Tyr, shouting over the music. Whetstone tried to shuffle sideways to hear better. A barrel-chested musician blew into a long battle horn, drowning out Thor's words with a sound like a cow mooing. Whetstone glared at him.

'Do you think that's what Odin is up to?' Tyr bellowed over the noise. 'Trying to get her out of Castle Utgard?'

Whetstone gasped. The harpist gave him a concerned look. Whetstone had heard of Castle Utgard. It was in Jotunheim: the Land of the Giants. That must be where his mother was. A grin broke out across Whetstone's face. He looked happily at Freyja, no longer resenting the feathery hat or the stupid trousers. He had just found out where his mother was and it had been SO easy! She quirked her eyebrows in return.

Thor shrugged. 'Maybe. I wouldn't mind taking a look for myself, though.' He hefted his hammer. 'I never miss the opportunity to see what the Giants are up to.'

Tyr laughed. 'When are you going?'

The battle horn blasted in Whetstone's ear again. He winced, his attention focused on Thor as he tried to lip-read the God's words.

Freyr shoulder-shimmied up to Thor and Tyr. In the

silence between mooing noises he asked, 'Not dancing, Thor? I bet you've got some moves.'

Tyr finished his cup of mead. 'Forget dancing – what we need is a good boast battle. Who wants to go first?'

Thor chuckled. 'Not me. I've not got the brains for the wordy stuff. The person you need is Loki.'

Whetstone shuddered. The battle horn nearly blasted all the feathers off his hat.

Carefully, Lotta stepped out of the kitchens. In her arms she carried an enormous silver plate with a giant cake, modelled to look like Freyja, balancing on top of it. Spotting the cake, Freyr whooped and danced away through the crowd, clearing a path for Lotta to a nearby table.

Freyja stood in the centre of the room, accepting everyone's birthday congratulations. The musicians struck up a new tune as the Gods sang, 'Happy birthday to you –'

The harp string round Whetstone's neck rang out. The blood seemed to freeze in the boy's veins. His chest felt tight.

The harp string's special power was to warn when danger was near.

'Happy birthday to you –'

Whetstone's eyes raked the crowd. Something *very* bad was about to happen.

'Happy birthday, dear Freyja –'

'Yeah Loki's who you're after.' Tyr chuckled. 'Where

is that slippery Fire Giant? He's never around when you want him!'

'Happy birthday to *you*!'

Freyja picked up a knife to make the first slice. 'I'd like to thank you all for coming—'

With a flash of green light, the door to Freyja's Great Hall was blasted into toothpicks. Gods and Goddesses dived out of the way as the air filled with dust and curling green smoke. The battle horn shot across the room. Freyja's birthday cake exploded, coating Lotta in icing and crumbs. Whetstone hit the ground, knocked sideways by the flute player. Whetstone peeked out, his heart hammering.

It couldn't be . . .

Amid the coughing and spluttering, all eyes were fixed on the doorway. A tall figure stepped inside.

'I'm sorry for not telling you I was coming, Freyja. My invitation must've gotten lost.' The smoke cleared to reveal a handsome man with collar-length blond hair wearing a red tunic.

Loki.

Whetstone tried to sink into the floor. A cake-smeared Lotta stared open-mouthed as a second figure appeared behind Loki.

Loki's son: Vali.

Author's Note

The children of Loki – what a *strange* bunch.

The most famous of Loki's children are Jormungandr, Fenrir and Hel. Odin believed that they would bring about the end of the Gods and tried to prevent this by separating them across the Nine Worlds. Spoiler alert: it didn't work.

Jormungandr, a poison-spraying sea serpent, was cast into the oceans of Midgard, where he grew so large that he could encircle the whole world. When Thor accidentally managed to pull him out of the water during a fishing trip, they became mortal enemies and it's said that they will destroy each other at Ragnarok.

Fenrir is a wolf whose rapid growth and incredible strength worried the Gods. According to legend, he will eventually be tricked and tied up in a magic ribbon. In retaliation, he bites off the hand of the God of Justice, Tyr. At Ragnarok, Fenrir will break free and get his revenge by swallowing Odin whole. Perhaps the Gods were right to be scared. I think I prefer my version of Fenrir, who is much fluffier.

Their sister, Hel, half-living-half-dead, rules over Helheim (translates as Hel's Home), a freezing land where the dead go to await Ragnarok. Not a place of punishment, but one of dullness and boredom. In the original stories, the Helhest was Hel's three-legged horse (she really does like naming things after herself), rather than the gooey shapeshifting creature in my book. The Hel's Belles are entirely my own (fabulous) invention.

Loki's most 'human' child is Vali. He only really pops up in Norse Mythology in connection with his very unpleasant ending, and as far as I know he is never turned into a Troll. In Scandinavian folklore, trolls are mountain-dwelling creatures who turn to stone when caught in the sunlight. They're unhelpful and dangerous loners – actually, they do sound a bit like Vali.

I am sure we will learn more about Loki's children in future stories.

Acknowledgements

This book was written under the less-than-brilliant conditions of lockdown, so I would like to thank all the keyworkers and everyone who kept the country ticking over during this difficult time.

A big thank you as always to my lovely family. To my husband, Steve, for bringing me cups of coffee, and to our daughters for letting me eat all the biscuits. A big thank you to my mum for always being supportive, even when she has no idea what I'm talking about.

I would also like to say thank you to my agent, Alice Williams, and the whole crew at Macmillan Children's Books for being endlessly enthusiastic. Sim, Lucy, Rachel, Sabina, Sarah, Cheyney and everyone else who has toiled away tirelessly to make *Land of Lost Things* a success.

Once again, a massive thank you to Katie Kear, for bringing the mad world of Whetstone and Lotta to life through your fabulous illustrations.

A final thank you goes to all the libraries, schools, bookshops, writing groups, and readers who have shown such love for *How to be a Hero*. You're all Heroes. No, honestly.

About the Author

Cat Weldon writes funny books for children and is a little bit obsessed with Vikings. With an MA in Scriptwriting, and a background in children's theatre, Cat has also worked as an English and Drama teacher – and in lots of other jobs where she can talk while waving her hands around wildly.

Cat Weldon now lives in East Anglia with her husband, daughters, and collection of delinquent chickens.

Although she has a favourite cup, it has never once recited poetry to her.

About the Illustrator

Katie Kear is a British illustrator and has been creating artwork for as long as she can remember.

Katie has an illustration degree from the University of Gloucestershire and has worked with publishers including Pan Macmillan, Penguin Australia, Andersen Press and Hachette. She is always on the hunt for brilliant stories to illustrate.

In her spare time she loves drawing, adventures in nature, chocolate, stationery, the smell of cherries and finding new inspirational artists!